IN THE SHADOW OF THE WITCH

BY
BRIAN WHITE

DARK-- REVELATIONS
Media LLC

DEDICATION

To my Holy Trinity: Gabi, Skye and Trinity, always dreaming, always believing.

IN THE SHADOW OF THE WITCH

CHAPTER 1

No sun could burn away the shadow of the witch. It darkened Trevor's heart, worming its way into the treasured deeps of his soul, stealing any hope of redemption. He could play spiritual chess in his head, trying to convince himself that when faced with insane circumstances in an insane world, the only available choices were insane and therefore his decisions could not be judged on a normal scale. But it was only a game, a lie he told himself when he felt the guilt and pain of his decisions. Life had placed him in check and he had chosen to foolishly try to play on instead of accepting that he had lost, every move bringing him closer to the end, pawns, knights and rooks sacrificed to his irrational belief in victory. But there was no winning in this game. His soul knew the truth of it; the dark epiphany he refused to acknowledge.

Trevor watched the boy, Kyle, from the safety of the woods, hiding behind a pine tree. He studied Kyle as he skipped rocks across the pond, an innocent toothy smile etched on his face, golden hair radiating in the glare of the sun. He was happy, enjoying the simple pleasure of skipping rocks on his way home from school. The boy was twelve, the same age as his son Jake. Trevor sighed, wondering how he would bring himself to do what needed to be done.

Jake's face superimposed itself on that of the boy. Jake was always smiling, even when he had learned of his imminent death. He had even tried to convince Trevor that everything would be alright. Trevor brushed a tear from his eyes, vision blurring as he rubbed. Kyle turned toward the forest, his back to the pond. The witch's head rose from the surface of the inky water, shattering it like glass as dark storm clouds rolled in overhead, lightning reflected in the fractured surface. Her larger left eye bulged outward blackly from the ash-gray, wrinkled, dead skin of her face. Crooked and cracked yellow teeth were exposed as her lips pulled back in a wicked sneer, completing a picture of insanity that filled him with dread. She raised her arms up over her head; long black curved nails, like the talons of a bird of prey reached to clutch the boy's shoulders and drag him below into the dark abyss.

Trevor shut his eyes, rubbed them with trembling fingers, and prayed to be delivered from this craziness. He opened his eyes. The witch was gone, the sun shone, buzzing insects flitted over the pond's surface, grains of pollen caught the rays of the sun, twinkling like dancing fireflies. The boy ran through the meadow back in the direction of the town. Trevor could only stare, petrified, unable to move. How could he do this? What kind of monster could even contemplate what he was planning? What dark pit of hell was reserved for someone capable of doing such a thing?

The witch reared up into his memory. That sly grin etched in stone on her face, the bulging evil black eye staring at him blankly, reflecting nothing, only consuming. Her voice echoes through the hall of his memory. "I can save him I can. But then you have to do something for me."

He had not even asked what. All he heard was "save him." There was nothing else. And how could he have known what she would want in return. But he should have. One look at the dead leathery skin, the black bulging left eye, the perpetual crooked leer, wild hair writhing as if each clumped greasy bundle was a ball of worms, the crazed look in her bloodshot right eye, and he should have known. Nothing sane could live in that face. Nothing good could come from its possessor. There was always a price to pay and the payment must fit the service rendered. The price for saving a life ... taking another.

Trevor watched as Kyle crested the hill. He knew the boy's parents, Sam and Jenny Waltham. He saw them at church on Sunday, whenever his wife dragged him. They had a reputation for helping anyone who asked and were considered valuable members of the community. Kyle was their only child, and Trevor could tell by their smiles and the light in their eyes whenever he saw them together that Kyle was the pride and joy of their lives. The Walthams were ranchers who lived on the outskirts of town past the old sun-reflecting field. At one time the reflecting field may have supplied the ranch and the rest of the town with power. But such things were now a mystery, their magic lost when the ancients who had built them passed on. Now it was just a field of glass panels that would, at times, catch the beauty of a sunrise or sunset in its mirrored surface. It was a place of superstition, a place to remember the stories of the ancients and their sorcery, nothing more. Trevor mused that Kyle would pass it on his way home, seeing the sunset reflected in its panes for maybe the last time in his life. What would he contemplate as he gazed into the reflection? Would a boy as young as he contemplate death, wonder what life had in store for him, or would he enjoy the moment the same way he had enjoyed skipping rocks across the surface of the pond, a simple innocent pleasure.

"I don't know if I can do this," he said for the thousandth time since the witch had told him the price for her assistance. He bowed his head and prayed for some divine resolution, even though he had never fully believed in God. But if something like the witch could exist, then other things he had thought impossible might exist as well. What would the consequences be for cheating the witch? He then wondered what further deal he could make, greasing the rungs of the ladder to hell with layers of unfulfilled promises. He was a simple blacksmith, he was no prophet, preacher, doctor, or politician, but surely even the witch had reason and would see the worth of a valuable trade.

But what did he have to offer? He had been told the Coma Witch only dealt in evil, nothing else. Money and possessions were nothing to her. She bargained only in pain, insanity, and death.

Trevor headed in the opposite direct of his escaping prey, toward the setting sun, toward home and Jake. And as he walked he felt confident in believing the worst that the witch could do was kill him ... but he was wrong.

When he entered the house, supper was on the table. The heady aroma of chicken broth and pepper greeted him at the door, followed quickly by the familiar scent of fresh-baked corn bread, which was a dinner staple that would always remind him of home. Such a pleasant smell would usually arouse his appetite, but today olfactory nostalgia crashed against the guilt and dread surrounding what he had contemplated doing not long ago, filling his stomach with acid, causing it to contract nauseously.

His son Jake smiled at him from across the table, a bread crumb hanging from the edge of his lip, "Daddy!" He quickly pushed his chair back and ran around the table to hug Trevor. His head was buried in father's chest; he had gotten so much taller this last year, despite the sickness. Despite ... Trevor felt cold, as he absently tousled Jake's brown hair and gave him a loving squeeze, momentarily able to block the horror from his mind.

Mary, his loving wife, the woman of his dreams, was next to him already, kissing his cheek gently, sending sparks down his throat to his chilled heart, attempting to warm it, revive it. He fought back tears as feelings of anger, terror, and hatred clashed against those of love and forgiveness. As he gazed into Mary's golden-brown eyes, he saw her concern and knew she had sensed his fear, his anguish.

"Why don't you sit down and eat with us honey. You've had a long day."

He moved to the head of the table silently and sat down, not trusting himself to speak, feeling that as soon as he opened his mouth the floodgates would open and he would be lost to sorrow.

Jake was too excited to notice anything was wrong, he spooned the chicken soup into his mouth while telling Trevor about his day at school, and recess, and his walk home, and his chores, and his homework, and … The stream became just a jumble of words that meant nothing to Trevor, but he so wanted them to. He wanted and longed to be caught in the simple banality of it. Conscious of Mary's wary eye examining him, Trevor feigned interest, nodding his head when he thought it appropriate, taking a small spoonful of the soup, which was tasteless and cold to his senses, swallowing, trying to smile, trying to make is seem like everything was alright as his world tipped and the cold and darkness set in.

Then supper was done, and Jake was reading by the light of the fire, and Mary was busily cleaning the table and then washing the dishes, and he observed it all as though it were theater, a play he had no role in, a mere spectator. And then he was kissing his son goodnight and looking in on his daughter Lydia who had been taking a long nap since late afternoon. He just wanted to see her, it seemed ages since this morning when she had raised her large brown toddler eyes to him and screamed *Dadda!* as he walked out the door.

Back in the living room Mary was waiting. She snatched his hand and led him out the door, across the yard to his shop, closing the door behind them and lighting a candle on the workbench where many of his steel-working tools were scattered. She gazed at him, concerned, fear danced within the darkness of her pupils spinning pirouettes in the candle light. She whispered conspiratorially, "What's wrong? Is it done?"

He could not meet the smoldering glare she leveled at him, which added frost to his heart. Where he would often look into those brown pools for warmth and compassion, he saw only accusation now. Everything had changed. One decision, one instant, and their lives would never be the same again.

"No," he whispered back, hearing the trembling in his voice in that one drawn-out syllable.

There was a fierceness to her gaze that he had never seen before and he wanted to look away. "This is for our son Trevor. It is for his safety. It was our bargain, our burden, the price we have to pay."

A mixture of pain and anger swirled within the cauldron of his emotions. She was accusing him of weakness, of being irresponsible, and worst of all, of not loving them enough to do what needed to be done. Her use of the word "our" fomented the anger seething below the surface, it had only been "ours" in the bargaining, when it came to the doing, to the paying up, it had been "yours," his. And now she was saying the failure, the cowardice, the guilt, was "his." Trevor wanted to know where the "ours" was in the woods as he was forced to watch the happy young boy skipping rocks, knowing all the while that he was scheming to kill him. Anger broke through the surface, pushing up against clenched teeth, but words began to leak out.

"We? Ours? And who has been saddled with the responsibility of payment, the task of taking another's life, an innocent boy's life. If you think it so easy, and me a cowardly fool, then by all means I will place the blade in your hands."

A tear shook from his eye, racking sobs quaking through his body, and he tried to pull back some control, the tempest of emotions swirling in and around him. "Why?" He put his hands over his face, shamed by his outburst, his tears. "Why Jake? Why her? Why us?" He was sobbing, but he forced himself to remove his hands and stare at her. His pain had broken through the icy layers she had been fortifying herself with, and he realized as he watched the transformation of her expression that she had been actively working on hardening her heart against feeling anything, or even questioning it. It was what had to be done, and there was nothing else to say or think. It was where they were.

The lines of her forehead smoothed, smoldering eyes cooled to warm empathy. With measured care and concern, holding back her own fear and sorrow, she spoke, "Why? Because life is unfair, because it is cruel. For so many reasons we'll never understand. But most of all, because we have a son that we said we'd do anything to save and now we are being asked to prove it."

She took his hand tenderly. Trevor took her into his embrace hugging her fiercely.

"And if we do this, do we become as evil as her?"

Rubbing the back of his neck staring soulfully into his eyes she whispered, "If we were capable of that you could have done this easily. Your pain and conflict is proof that we don't have the seed of such evil in us. Do this and we can be whole again. Please."

He kissed her neck but made no reply. He thought she was wrong. Once you let that darkness in, there would be no means of pushing it out and it would transform them bit by bit, like the rust that transforms the very makeup of iron, changing its very nature until it is not iron anymore but rust, losing its form, changed beyond the ability to repair. That is what had happened to the ancients and to their world. Now it was happening to him.

That night he dreamed of the witch and the event that led to the bargain.

He had entered the house to find his wife sitting at the table. Jake looked up at him, eyes wide in horror and shock, his large pupils reflecting the leathery, creased face hovering in front of him, one eye bulging outward, eye reflecting eye in an infinite loop. In dream space the reflection multiplied to infinity, swirling and spiraling, that awful stare becoming a force of nature, a physical void that swallowed all of reality.

The house was hot, the fire burning fiercely in the hearth, beads of sweat standing out on Jake's forehead becoming crystallized, firelight danced and refracted in the larger droplets, becoming hundreds of eyes that glowed orange and red as they ran down his cheeks, staring in all directions. His face reddened, the skin stretching, falling downward off his skull, melting like wax in the heat.

They had learned a few months earlier that within Jake's body some dark anomaly had pumped poison into his blood and was killing him. The disease and its poison had no name. The village doctor, Doctor Talbot, had no cure or explanation only a prognosis based on previous experience; painful and certain death.

On some command mumbled by the witch, Jake opened his mouth wide, the tunnel of his throat opening to the horror of the world in a silent scream, the witch turned her enlarged left eye to stare into the cavern, mumbling softly as she studied the depths.

His wife, finally noticing Trevor's arrival, turned to him and got up. She leaned in and whispered conspiratorially in his ear, "I called on her. She is our last hope." They had talked of this. Where did one go when all logical options were exhausted? Legends and magic. Everyone in Devon knew of the witch and what she could do. There were only stories and speculation surrounding what the price for her talents was. At the time, a decision to call on her seemed harmless, but with her here, so close, her darkness sucking the light out of the room, he no longer thought her presence benign.

The witch turned and Trevor had to stifle a cry that rose in his throat. He did not think he kept the surprise from registering on his face. She looked like a corpse: ashen, cracked, leathery skin; thick veins pulsed within jaundiced sclera surrounding a transparent icy blue iris; cracked and twisted yellow teeth protruded from black gums; thin lips were drawn back in a rictus of insanity. She was a hag with a large black left eye that projected out toward him as if pressure from within the gelatinous mass was telescoping its blackness toward him.

Suddenly this was not just a last-ditch effort. Trevor felt her dark power, knew that such a black force had the capability to control and command all the dark things in the world, Jake's dark passenger among them. It was wonderful. It was terrible. It was hope. It was everlasting despair. He was shivering in the heat of the room.

The Coma Witch trailed a long legend filled with the types of unbelievable stories he now knew were true. She was staring at him with that obsidian eye, his reflection trapped and morphed momentarily in its surface and then summarily annihilated till there was only the lifeless black.

"Aye, I cans take the poison in him away." Her voice was deep, reverberating in the air, drumming against his ears. The air shifted around her words, intensifying their meaning, their power. Had she read his thoughts? Answered a question he had not yet voiced aloud?

"But then you must do something for mees."

He could only nod. There was only the cold, only the dark. He felt nothing as he condemned his family to hell.

The nest of her hair danced in the firelight, snakes writhing, the mythic gorgon turning his heart to stone with a glance as she spoke. "You won'ts know what the thing will be nor whens it will come. But whens I ask, you must do ..." each word slithered over the previous, punctuated with a hiss. She paused, staring at him fixedly, pulling apart his soul as he stood their petrified by her gaze, "or else."

Else would be awful, torture, he had no need to ask, and knew she would not answer. Her terror lay in darkness and mystery, his mind supplying the dark imaginative scenarios she would put him through, each successive vision more terrible than the previous one. This was not a negotiation. The terms had been set. Trevor could either agree and save his son or allow him to die knowing he could have saved him.

"What'll it be, aye or nay? You needs speak it—a nod won't do."

Somewhere in the back of his mind there was the realization that saying *yes* meant annihilation, that it would set in motion a course of events far worse than the death of his son. But at the time he could contemplate no greater wrong than the death of his innocent son.

"Yes!" Trevor choked out before his mind could question it anymore. "Yes. I accept your offer."

"Aye. Very well then."

The witch turned back to Jake, "Stand in front of me boy and open your mouth a little. This wills feel strange but don'ts you struggle. Thats will only make it hurt."

Jake nodded, obviously scared but trying to be brave.

The Coma Witch leaned in, her hair eclipsing Jake's face as she placed her ashen, cracked lips on Jake's. He could hear the sucking of air as she breathed in forcefully. She seemed to enlarge, becoming twice her size, skin turning to shadow, looming over her prey, ready to consume. In the slowness of dream time Trevor saw something he had previously missed. As she eclipsed Jake, obscuring Trevor's vision of him, she had delicately pushed her hand against Jake's shoulder, her hand twisted to conceal what she carried there. She squeezed at something and then let her hand drop to her side, her fist clenched, disappearing into her tattered robe. What had it been? Ancient medicine? Had the rest been nothing more than a show to conceal this simple act? And then it was over. A slow exhalation, shrinking, the air normalizing, the nightmare over.

Jake's eyes were glassy, his head bobbed on his neck like a puppet. He sat down dizzily, clutching at the armrest of the chair to keep himself from falling. Mary ran to him and put her arm around his shoulder, cupping his head to her breast, stroking his hair and face. The witch observed him thoughtfully, her eye roving up and down his body. She let out a loud burp and sniffed at the air thoughtfully, searching the scent for something.

"You be fine boy. Lay downs and rest. In the morning you feels good as a newborn babe."

She stood up and approached Trevor, her icy shadow freezing him in place. His muscles quaked at her approach, stomach lurched in his throat, every fiber of his being tried to crawl away, and in that ever-expanding revulsion there was the clarity of thought that told him his soul had just been forfeited. She touched his cheek, one sharp nail of her finger trailing his jaw line. Skin crawled under the slug mucus touch that burned in the finger's wake like acid. She did not speak with her mouth but directly into his mind, the neurons wired to hear dark miracles responded to the call of her black epiphany.

"Yous come whens I call. You do whats I ask. No exceptions."

She seemed to pass through him. Suddenly just gone. His heart pounding as his mind replayed her words, "No exceptions."

In the dream he heard laughter followed by silence and darkness.

The next day Jake was fine, healed. Running around, playing like he had not done in months. The fever, nausea, and cramps had kept him in bed most days. But on that day he could not be kept in bed or in the house. He ran to school, played with the other children, and reveled in the simplicity of being a child who no longer had a death sentence hanging over him. Trevor forced himself to smile, told himself to be happy, to be grateful, but there was a shadow cast upon everything now. It was on that day that Trevor's soul sickness began, as he waited for her call, which arrived three months later.

She had used the same dark magic to reach into his mind, speaking to those receptors now wired to her voice. The dark recesses of his mind conjured a phantom smoky image of her as she spoke. She showed him a young boy, twelve or so, blue eyes, blonde hair, handsome, smiling, full of life.

"Sees this boy?"

"Yes."

"You knows him don't ye?"

"Yes. His name is Kyle."

"He needs be dead. And you needs kill him."

He was shaking his head.

"No exceptions, remember. No exceptions."

Scenes of blood spattering a wall, a baby screaming. The sound of flesh hitting flesh, dead, lifeless, wet smacking. Bones cracking, the sounds worse than the blood, filling his head and whirling around like a tempest. "No exceptions." She cackled as the images repeated, her black eye the theater for this repeating murder scene. Screaming now, "NO EXCEPTIONS!" Her evil laughter following him down the tunnel of unconsciousness.

His eyes flicked open, a scream caught in his throat, choking him, rancid sweat covering his body, "No exceptions," he whispered into the darkness.

Chapter 2

That afternoon, with the echoes of the nightmare tormenting and driving him, Trevor followed Kyle to the woods again. Trevor was not a graceful or stealthy man and knew he would be unable to sneak up effectively on the boy. He briefly wondered why Kyle came this way from school, since his home lay in the opposite direction. But it was nothing more than a curiosity; never becoming for him a mystery that begged an answer.

He had played the horrid scene through in his mind thousands of times.

"Kyle!"

The boy stopped in his tracks and turned. Something seemed wrong, Trevor could see the flash of recognition cross Kyle's face, but there was still this look of surprise as if he had been caught doing something he was not supposed to be doing or was just about to do. His flesh flashed crimson, his voice quavered slightly, "Mr. Williams?"

Trevor walked slowly toward him trying to seem innocent, nonthreatening. The knife was clutched in his sweating palm, hidden behind his back. Practicing the scene in his mind he would step up to the boy and when it was time to kill he would slash with his right hand toward the boy's throat, but in this phantom practice the blade never connected, the sequence stopping and fading to black before the moment of truth arrived. If he could not complete the task in a thought experiment, in fantasy practice, how was he going to bring himself to do it now, in reality, where it counted?

The boy's eyes were huge as he gazed up at Trevor, lips quivering slightly. Why was he afraid? The boy knew him, knew Jake, his family. Did his evil intent scar the air, projecting his ugly purpose as he approached?

"Mr. Williams?" his voice quavered as he begged confirmation not of Trevor's identity, but of his intent.

The boy continued to stare at him, now looking terrified, his mouth agape, the unspoken questions hanging in the air: *Why? Why did you stop me? Why are you looking at me like that? What are you going to do Mr. Williams?*

There was only one answer, "I'm sorry, Kyle."

He meant to raise the knife, but he found his arm had turned to stone. Sweat poured from his forehead, he clenched his teeth with the effort of trying to will his arm to move, to obey his mind's simple command. Or maybe it was following a deeper intent far below the level of conscious direction, that mystical place that knew universal truth, right and wrong. He pictured Jake in his mind, pictured him with pale dead skin, pictured the witch hovering over him, putting her disgusting lips to his and removing her cure. "No exceptions."

But he could not move.

"Sorry, Kyle. I just saw you and yelled out impulsively. I didn't mean to frighten you. You can go. Say hello to your mom and pop for me please."

"Aye, I shall Mr. Williams." He still looked scared. Then, most likely out of habit, he added the local blessing, "And to you and yours, good fortune."

Trevor nodded and responded in kind, "And to you and yours, good fortune."

Everything about the scene felt odd. Forced. Two actors on a stage fidgeting uncomfortably, just trying to exit stage left with as much dignity as possible. Trevor nodded goodbye, and Kyle turned and ran deeper into the forest, still going in the opposite direction from his home, but Trevor was too distraught to notice or question. He began to cry, wondering what he would tell his wife or Jake. There had to be a way to fix this and escape the witch with their lives intact.

His eyes were still red-rimmed from tears as he walked past his shop. He briefly thought how he would have to take care of some business soon or the witch would not be the only person coming after him to retrieve an owed debt. There were horseshoes and axles that needed to be worked on lying in an orderly pile on various workbenches. Knowing what he was going through with Jake, the villagers had been kind, but that could not last much longer. It also helped that he had been willed one of the ancient fire-cutting tools by his grandfather, which meant his work was often quicker, more precise, and longer lasting. He knew of no other blacksmiths with access to such a tool. But this advantage only added a week or so to his customer's patience, they relied on these things in their daily lives and would not be able to do without much longer. Their patience had been a form of empathy and kindness, and he appreciated it.

He paused to glance through the shop's open doors, the hearth cold, his tools hanging from hooks on a peg-board, the sound of hammer falling on steel and anvil ringing in his memory as he gazed at them lying before the hearth covered in dust. For a moment, worrying about work, making money, paying bills, normal life situations that others concerned themselves with, he felt a moment of peace. Maybe this would all work out and they could go back to their simple existence without the threat of death, contemplating murder, and escaping the witch. There was the shadow of a smile on his face when he opened the front door of the house.

He stood upon the threshold, his hand on the doorknob, his eyes gazing upon a scene that his mind refused to compute. It was complete chaos, a patchwork of destruction, blood everywhere, flesh lying in torn pieces creating a shattered puzzle all around him. Everywhere he looked there was some horror to alight on. And the smell, it assaulted his senses, turning his stomach, bile rising in his throat. He retched and threw up. Eyes watering, he could not seem to breathe, his heart pounding in his ears, his vision folding in blackly around him.

The lifeless eyes of Jake, Mary, and baby Lydia stared at him, freezing him in place. Their heads lay on the dinner table turned to face the door so as to greet him with lifeless horror as he entered. Their dismembered bodies created the tapestry of flesh, organs, blood, and bile that littered the main room. Blood sizzled in the embers of the fire, pieces of fat, skin, and sinew smoking on the hearth creating the noxious air that threatened to tip him into unconsciousness.

They stared at him, pleading for redemption. The black tunnel of shock was squeezing his reality into a tight cylinder. It was just a nightmare, he told himself, it could not be real. Those three pairs of eyes became accusatory as the witch whispered in his mind, "No exceptions."

"Why couldn't you do this one thing for us?" His wife asked.

"You let me die, Daddy. I thought you loved me."

Lydia only whimpered softly, somehow so much worse than a verbal accusation. Her innocence in all this, just wanting to live, to be protected.

"Why Daddy? Why?"

"Was Kyle's life worth more than ours? Was your morality worth more than our lives?"

Sobbing uncontrollably, "I'm sorry. How could I have known what she'd do? How?"

"You're a coward. A self-righteous coward, Trevor!"

The blackness squeezed in, he screamed in pain, in agony, in the hope that the darkness would claim him completely and it would all be over. He fainted, falling into a sea of blood, vomit, bile, and flesh.

The nightmare did not end there. No, that was just the beginning. It was merely the call of the witch.

Chapter 3

It was Sam Neilson who had been the unfortunate friend to find this bloody tableau. He had been waiting two weeks for Trevor to fix his wheel and axle. Sam had decided he could not wait any longer and had come to call on Trevor only to find a scene that a lifetime could never erase. When Sam had first happened upon the scene, he had assumed the whole family was dead. Trevor had been rolling through the gore while being tortured by delirium nightmares. In those nightmares the witch had wormed her way into his mind, possessed Trevor, and forced him to kill his family and dismember them. In the repeating nightmare he had struggled against her invasion but she had won. As he was forced to watch the scene behind his own possessed eyes, he had no doubt that what he saw was what had actually happened, the disembowelment, the beheading, and then the witch's black magic keeping them alive until that instant when he had walked through the door so that they could accuse him of cowardice. This was the nightmare she used to poison his mind so that he would know exactly what had happened and see the scene as she had seen it, feel his loved ones' last painful thoughts as they gazed upon him, the hurt, the resentment, the sorrow at a life cut short, all the things they would never do, the confusion as they saw their father/husband enter the house, wondering why he was alive, why, if he had done as the witch had asked, they were not all sitting down to supper together? Why? All these emotions and questions rushed through him simultaneously, crushing him with the weight of their collective despair.

He now knew they had been tortured. Dying had been a welcome release that they had begged and screamed for in their pain-filled minds. He would never be able to lie to himself and believe that she had killed them quickly, only staging the rest of the scene to punish him. No, they had been able to feel it all, the agony intensified beyond human comprehension by the witch's magic, keeping them alive as she exposed every neuron to pain. Then she had directed that black magic at him, spilling the stored poison of her vision into the dark synapses of his mind to ensure he knew the truth in excruciating detail. The truth of what his morality and defiance had cost.

While in the throes of these nightmares he had crawled and rolled in the gore and blood of his family, camouflaged in death when Sam had arrived at his door to check on his wheels and axle. Sam had taken a single wide-eyed gawking glance and fled, vomiting, as he ran toward town to get the sheriff.

The sheriff, Peter Miller, could not understand anything that Sam blathered except that something had happened at the Williams's residence. Sam's skin was white, quivering blue lips tried to form words but were incapable of the task. But it was enough. It was Peter that found Trevor deliriously moaning and writhing on the floor covered in blood. He screamed as Peter pulled him from the house, "The witch killed them!"

The rest was a hazy blur to Trevor. His mind was swarmed and eclipsed by sorrow and death, and in their wake budding hatred for both himself and the witch. He could take revenge upon himself easily enough but not before he took justice on the witch and tortured her the way she had his family.

Three coffins lay side by side. The air was cold, damp, and gray. Jeff Halstead the undertaker had never seen such a death. But the family deserved his best. They deserved to be at peace. He had been sick many a times and doubted the images would ever be cleared from his mind, but he had done what he could with the bodies so that Trevor could be at peace with their final resting and be assured that they had been treated with reverence and respect. Trevor had thanked him, but Jeff saw that the man would never be right again. How could he be? To get over something like that one would have to be more or less than human. He had known Trevor for a long time, a down-to-earth fellow, dependable and very human. He felt sorry for him. But cleaning up the remains, attempting to sort the parts into the correct caskets, trying to stitch them back into some semblance of humanity was most likely the best he would ever be able to do for Trevor. The man was beyond human hope and help.

The coffins were laid in their holes. The priest said words that Trevor heard but could not make sense of, something about the grace of God and never understanding his grand plan. There would be anger, hate, questioning, but these were of the devil and hell. Now was the time for faith. He reminded everyone that the ancients had sought a life free of pain and hardship and had attempted to build their own heaven. They had destroyed everything in the process while removing themselves from God's grace. Life was about learning from pain and seeking God when in the midst of turmoil and darkness.

At home sitting before the vacant fireplace he could still smell them, their blood stained the wood of the floor, of the walls, of his heart. Everywhere he looked their ghosts smiled at him. For a moment he could feel their love and kindness, replaced by hurt and accusation in the next instant. Their gossamer forms would reach out to him in despair and he would try to comfort them, to hold them one last time and reassure them he was going to make it all right again. But the phantoms disappeared at his touch only to reappear later and begin the cycle all over again.

It was only a few days after the funeral that he came to the realization that he could not stay in the house. He could not die yet, and staying here was killing him. The souls of his family could not rest until he took vengeance upon the witch, and he could not contemplate how to accomplish that while haunted by their ghostly presence.

That night he started the fire in his shop for the first time since meeting the witch and making the deal. He then removed the fire cutter from its hiding place beneath a loose floor board. He had no idea what magic powered it. His grandfather, upon giving it to him, had told him that one day its energy would run out and he had no understanding of how to refill it, so he had told Trevor to use it sparingly. As he pulled the trigger at its base, a red cylinder of flame leaped from the tip. He was not here to mend horseshoes or repair broken axles. Instead, he began to make a series of blades, daggers, scimitars, saw-toothed, short, long, straight, bowed, a spear like a whale harpoon with a razor-sharp blade and barbs for extra damage. Carefully he ran the fine beam across steel, following the pattern he had etched in pencil to create the shape of his weapons. The point cut through the metal with ease, requiring no effort, and was exact, allowing him to create the intricate designs produced by his fevered brain.

The tears and sweat born of pain and rage were pounded into the metal, an alchemical transformation that turned his previously moderate skill and work into true works of art, their edges astounding, their points so fine as to be invisible, capable of splitting the molecules of darkness. Metal was folded, refolded, honed to perfection, the best work he had ever done. His rage and despair had focused him in a way pride and money never had, turning a mediocre blacksmith into an artist who created beautiful and deadly weapons.

He was in the shop for more than two weeks, leaving only to gather and split more wood for the forge. He slept beneath one of the workbenches close to the fire and would wake and begin work again. He took no food, only water. There was some process at work within him that he could feel but not understand, as if he were being molded and shaped in the same way the metal was being transformed by the heat of the flames and the pounding of his hammer. The sweat was cleansing, fasting removed softness, the hardening of metal hardened his heart; the process of forging weapons paralleled the forging of his body and soul into a tool of destruction. He thought of his dead trinity less and less, and pictured the face of the witch more and more, focusing on becoming an instrument of darkness and hate capable of delivering justice to the witch.

His body hardened and strengthened under the constant stress of hammering on the anvil, cutting trees, splitting wood, carrying logs, or pulling a sled burdened with hundreds of pounds of split wood for the fire. When he slept, his mind filled with the techniques for molding the iron and steel, it showed him the shapes of the weapons, how they could be used and once he was done with the weapons his mind filled with magical symbols and alphabets and phrases he knew nothing about but was determined to etch into the steel.

Beyond the pain his mind would clear and he would remember lessons and stories his father and grandfather had told him about the ancients and their sorcery, which they had called "science and techknowledgy." Their brand of magic had scarred the world, giving birth to true darkness. They had talked of invisible dark and light forces controlled by mystics and witches armed with weapons crafted by their science. There were tales of mutants and ghosts, experiments gone wrong that had created wastelands in the far corners of the world, breeding demons. Father had pointed out the sun fields and the machines that lay rotting and lifeless in the woods and fields and there was always some cautionary tale associated with them. Father had told him he believed that man in his attempt to understand God had then decided he could become God and then proceeded to destroy the world with his unbridled egotism. They only wanted to explore what they could, never asking whether they should. In the wake of these memories, the sigils of this ancient science would fill his mind, and he would heat the metal to molten red and carve the runes and symbols into the transformed metal. Just as he was finishing the etchings on his last weapon, the cutting tool stopped working, the beam of light winking out. No matter how many times he pulled the trigger, shook it, flicked the lever on and off, the beam never reappeared. It was done. He threw it aside. He was finished anyway. It was now just another ancient tool that had run down and run out. There were so few left.

After a few weeks he was done. He then spent a few more weeks training, running in the woods, slashing at branches with his new weapons, throwing the harpoon, carrying heavy stones uphill, his mind vacant, the strain and effort pushing his body beyond what he would have thought possible. Whenever he thought he could take no more, the witch's face would appear as she cackled, "No exceptions." And then she would decapitate one of the trinity. Lydia was always the worst to bear but he would continue to fight, his body now a machine under the control of a mind warped by the need for vengeance and fueled by the darkness of hate. Those images became black strokes of paint on a canvas that was now almost completely dark. He was becoming a void.

He filled a rucksack with some food and a canteen of water. He had killed a dear, a bear, and two wolves during his training. The wolves he had dispatched in close quarters with daggers and they had taken a few flesh-and-blood trophies of their own, skin from one calf and deep cuts on his bicep, before he had slit their throats. It was part of his transformation. He wanted everything he was to be new, to be transformed into this new engine of hate and redemption. The skins from these kills were his wardrobe, their blood his baptism. It was time to move on, entering a new dimensional sphere of reality.

He had crafted a sling for his weapons and scabbards that hung from various straps and clips concealed by the bearskin coat; short daggers dangled from his hip and were strapped to his legs. When he moved nothing bounced, he was silent, floating swiftly through space, more shadow than man. He took a log that he had left smoldering in the fire of the forge and set his workbenches ablaze. He then moved out of the shop and stood in the open doorway of the house. The house where he had learned of love, love for a wife, the unconditional love of children, the contentment of home. Those memories were there, hanging before him in an ethereal cloud, replaying history in a schizophrenic puzzle sequences that could no longer form a cohesive picture.

A tear tried to remind him he was still human. It spilled from the corner of his eye and ran hotly down his cheek, etching a line of pain down his face. He did not wipe it away as he swore it would be the last tear he would shed until the witch was dead. At the time he believed there was nothing left to lose. He was wrong. It was a promise he would not be able to keep.

He touched the torch to the bedcovers and watched them flare up. A phantom of his wife rose from a restless sleep, staring at him confused. Turning away he set the curtains ablaze. He backed out the front door and threw the log into the middle of the floor beneath the table that had contained the decapitated heads of his family. Their ghosts stood on the far side of the table. They were smiling, tears in their eyes, relieved, released, waving goodbye. He backed up further as the rising flames erased them and the heat began to scorch and burn his skin.

He did not know how long he stood there. The house had burned to the ground, the timbers steaming in the morning cold. He took a handful of the ash and placed it in a tin box, closed the lid, and walked off into the forest heading west, following her. He and the witch had become connected in some way during his transformation, and Trevor could feel her energy pulling at him, guiding him to her. It felt to him like a form of gravity, a strange inexplicable force that was subtle but easily recognizable once he became attuned to it. They were linked by this dark energy and he would never be free of it unless he severed it.

The witch visited him in his dreams, cackling, goading him on with visions and reminders of what she had done to his family. In the morning he would wake huddled within a cave or the hollow of a tree, the reek of pine and cedar smoke from the smoldering fire filling his nostrils. The tendrils of night hung in the air, swirling around him, and there would be her phantom face staring at him from a plume of thick smoke lit and formed by the first rays of a dawn sun, her evil eye pulling at him. He could feel that stare in the pit of his stomach. It was at times a purely physical reaction, a muscle or body memory that was not spurred by his emotional reaction to her appearance. She had awoken or stirred some ancestral, primordial genetic memory that rose through his entire being, a visceral awareness leading to awakening.

In the hills the air was cold and still, the morning dew turning to frost and as her diaphanous face floated away, torn apart by the rays of the sun and dispersed, he would look out upon pristine forest, ice crystals covering patches of moss as if magically floating just above the ground, stalactite icicles hanging from the low branches of the trees catching the first flickers of sun, twinkling like jewels, sweating spiderwebs icing in the cold, interlinking the larger formations to create a world of dazzling ice; a cathedral of cold beauty. There was a modicum of peace to be found in these brief moments of magnificence. At these times he would picture Jake smiling or laughing. He would remember the feel of Mary's body beneath him, the clean smell of her skin, the unblemished perfection of it, soft to the touch, sweet to his lips.

With the sun shining on his face, the ghost of a smile on his lips, for a fleeting second he would question what he was doing. Was this for them? Or was it for him? To free him of guilt, to fill his need for blood, an eye for an eye vengeance? Had the witch awakened something deep and dark within him that suddenly wanted to indulge in this chase of violence and evil? That needed it the way he used to need the love of his wife and children?

In his youth he had been intrigued by philosophy and metaphysics. His father had always been one to pose existential questions: *Why are we here? Is there a God? Did the two primary and elementary particles of darkta and illukta have a soul or purpose? Was the darkta under the influence of a dark god and the illukta the tool of a god of light, or were they the opposed yet balancing aspects of one God?* They would bandy these questions about, enjoying the mental gymnastics that in the end were nothing more than a pleasant dance. There was no utility to be found in it. Their joy was only in the questioning, in the searching and seeking. His father was a learned, loving man, and would talk philosophy with anyone who would listen. He was a terrible carpenter, but his customers hired him just so they could talk and listen to what he had to say or to solicit advice. They knew he could not cut a straight line or hang a door that would not be crooked and creaking, but they loved him and knew that if they did not pay him he would be forced to move on and they did not want that. Funny as it seemed, his father had really been a traveling monk who went from house to house to give his knowledge and advice. Trevor loved him and always looked up to him. He had died of a failed heart ten years earlier and the village had never been the same since.

But even years before his death Trevor had ceased enjoying knowledge for knowledge sake. At some point he had become a man of utility and ceased to see the joy or purpose of such questions. He had taken up the trade of blacksmithing, taught to him by his grandfather, who died only three years prior to his father. His grandfather was more the dreamer, reveling in myths and stories of the ancients. At the time Trevor had no more use for these than he had for his father's philosophy, but they helped pass the time as they worked or took breaks.

He now found himself contemplating how pertinent these conversations and stories had become to his life. The questions posed by his father, the morals of the tales told by his grandfather suddenly seemed grave, more important. Finding the answers to them could impact his existence, his next actions. If he had a soul, if his family had souls, could they still be saved? Was there redemption for any of them? Did the witch control darkta or did it control her? If it controlled her was she to blame for her actions? And then what controlled her? God? To find vengeance, to bring peace to his soul, would he have to kill God? Was that possible?

All of this would occur to him in a flash during these quiet moments, and then the sun would move, and that miraculous moment would be over, and the questions would pass unanswered; he would toss dirt on the remaining embers of the fire and put his few belongings back in his rucksack and head west on his continued pilgrimage. Upon reflection, the why of it did not even matter, because he did not know what else he would do if he failed to follow this path. He had no other purpose, no other direction. He chased the witch's shadow without thought as to what his true goal was or whether he was following fate or challenging it.

The first village he encountered came a week after he had left the ruins of his smoldering house. Krull was not much more than a few weathered buildings—saloon, general store, blacksmith, granary, bank—all leaning over the dirt track of Main Street as if the tops of the structure were being pulled toward that centerline, keeping it in perpetual shadow. At the road's terminus stood a white church, black shutters hanging askew like broken teeth in a crooked grin. Behind the church was a ghost-talk tower, its twisted steel rising into the air, the rectangular boxes circling its apex pointed toward the ground. His father had informed him that the boxes created signals that were vibrated into the air, where they could be received and turned into voices by little boxes people had once carried with them or stuck in their ears. The thought gave him a chill as he imagined what it would be like to hear disembodied voices whispering into his head. The tower loomed as a monument to chaos, darkness, and fear. His grandfather had always told him that when things went bad for the ancients and their inventions turned against them a strange paradox occurred, what they had called "ghost towns" had become the habitat for the survivors of the technopocalypse and the techno cities had become the halls of the dead. In most villages that people ran to, far away from the techno cities and dark magic that was poisoning the world, only the ghost-talk towers or the sun fields existed. They stood as monuments and reminders of what could happen when man began to think too much of himself. At least that was how grandfather had always spun it.

At the general store he got some jerky, bread, and salted bacon. The store owner had watched him as he had selected his purchases. Not warily, just curiously. He probably did not encounter many outsiders, as Krull was a way station to nowhere, further west there were only forest and the mountains and beyond those the mythic wasteland. He placed his items on the counter. "I've been chasing a woman I think passed through here."

The store owner now took him in, looking him up and down without pretense or shyness. "Trevor, I presume?"

Trevor tried not to look dismayed, but hearing his name from the mouth of someone he had never met had a way of unsettling him, and he coiled for attack, believing that was what would follow. Confusion washed across his face, his eyes staring, his body going into instant alarm.

"She was here alright. Said she had a message for you." He paused as if waiting for something. Trevor had rarely left his small hamlet of Devon. He had led a quiet life free of adventure. His definition of a long journey was a two-day wagon ride to Hashen for steel or other supplies. The social mores and code of ethics of such silence was lost on him. The air was charged with expectation but what it expected he could not discern.

"The message?"

Being more direct, seeing his silence was not understood, the owner put out his hand, "Information costs, just like all else here in Krull. Everything has a price."

This surprised Trevor more than the fact that the witch had left him a message. At first he was tempted just to pay and be done with it. But suddenly he felt anger rise up in him, followed immediately by defiance.

"If she gave you a message then she also put a condition upon its delivery. So if you don't deliver it the cost will be on you to pay."

The man swallowed hard, seeing the steely look in Trevor's eyes. His words were delivered behind clenched teeth, barely contained rage vibrated just below the surface of his skin. The owner withdrew his open hand and rubbed his balding head. His head turned from left to right, his eyes scanning the interior as if he expected the witch to suddenly appear. Trevor had been correct. There was a curse waiting in the wings if this opportunistic weakling did not do as he had been told.

"She says ..." he paused. "Sorry," he apologized, now visibly nervous, his hands shaking, voice quavering, sweat beading on his brow. "She said this must be delivered word for word. She made me memorize it and repeat it for her before she would leave, so I'll say it slow." Trevor nodded, willing him to just get it out. He disliked this weasel of a man but showing contempt, frightening him, or displaying annoyance would only hinder the delivery.

"Catching me will be more than just catching up to me. This is an ancient and perilous ritual you embark upon and the man that starts the journey won't be the same man that finishes it. Be sure this is what you want." He paused for a moment going through the lines as he bobbed his head and used his index finger as though he were viewing the words in the air before him. Then he gazed up at the cracked ceiling for inspiration. "There is a mountain directly west named Blood Mountain by my kind and kin. Once you cross its summit, if you do cross its summit, I will consider you on the quest and then there is no turning back. This interaction of ours will then be grave and only one of us shall survive. So it is. So it has been. Be warned. Be prepared."

The words offered a cryptic warning and named his next destination, Blood Mountain, but offered little else that he could understand.

"Is that it?"

The man shook his head, gulped and took a cautionary step back, wanting to be out of Trevor's immediate reach, "And go fuck yourself and your family! She'd always laugh after that part but I can't reproduce it thankfully."

"No need I know its sound well enough. Had you seen her before that?"

"No but the priest saw her leaving and said he knew of her."

Trevor turned to leave. He wanted to be away from the man, he found himself suppressing a desire to reach across the counter, grab him, and then punch his sniveling face to pulp. Over his shoulder he muttered, "Pray you never see the witch or I again."

Father Roberts wore the dress of a priest—black pants, black shirt, black jacket, and a scapula around his neck—but other than these there was nothing in his look that defined him as a holy man. Roberts had long salt-and-pepper hair leaning more toward salt. It hung past his shoulders in unkempt strands. One side of his face was obscured by greasy strands of hair that hung down in front of it. He had hooked the hair behind his left ear so that he could see his drink, Trevor guessed. He had seen the man hobble into the saloon, and since it was on the way to the church, he thought he would follow the priest inside and save himself an unnecessary trip.

"You the priest in this town?" Trevor asked as he sat down next to Roberts at the bar.

Robert's eyes turned to glance sideways but he was not interested enough to turn his head, "Aye, that's what they call me. The only service people seem to attend around here are funerals and even then you're only guaranteed one attendee who ain't even listening." He gave a wry smile, and Trevor found himself liking the man. At least he did not seem like the snake the store owner had been.

The bartender walked over to the men, "Drink?"

Trevor tried to wave him away but the man stared at him, digging in. Again Trevor had missed the subtext. It was not a question of whether he would have a drink, it was what he would have to drink. With a stern look, the bartender clarified, "This ain't no sitting parlor. You drink or you walk."

"I'll have what he's having."

The bartender rolled his eyes, which seemed odd to Trevor until he put the amber liquid in front of him and Trevor took a sip and smiled, "Apple juice?"

The priest smiled crookedly at him, "I'm not here to lose myself. I'm here to find myself."

"Then this is to finding ourselves," Trevor lifted his glass, and the priest tapped it with his own, and they both drank.

It had been some time since Trevor had spent time with another person and for a moment he felt human again, something he had not felt since the witch had come into his life.

"So. What brings the likes of you to a saloon, looking for a priest, drinking apple juice in search of himself."

Trevor tried to return a grin but it felt wrong on his face. "I'm in pursuit of someone who passed through here and the general store owner said you may know something of her."

The priest rolled his eyes. "Cyrus, that rat-faced liar. He try to hustle you?"

"Aye."

"Sorry."

Trevor shrugged "No harm done. You don't know of her then?"

"The witch?" Trevor nodded. "Aye, I do. I was just commenting that Cyrus is a rat-faced liar in general but he told you true regarding the witch. I know of her. I know something of the lives she's ruined with her curses and deals. She is darkness, a black destructive annihilating force of nature."

"Do you know anything more? What she really is? What she's done to others?"

"Why?"

"She made a deal with me and I couldn't hold up my end. So she murdered my family." He delivered his story in a factual fashion. He did not want to feel it and told himself he would not. Not one more tear would he shed in her name, he had sworn.

The priest was shaking his head, eyes moist. "Much like the stories I've heard from others. It ends bad either way, mister. You do what she wants and then you can't live with it or that causes some other event that creates a catastrophe. That one there is a catastrophizer. And as difficult as it may be to hear, the truth is that one way or the other your family was most likely going to die."

He paused and took a sip of his juice. Trevor waited.

"I've heard her called the Coma Witch. Folks say that after she's been in your life you go through the rest of it as if you are in a coma. It's not real living. Don't matter what she gives, what she takes, or what you do, life just won't be what it was once she been in your life and in your head."

Trevor nodded his agreement.

The priest looked at him with slate-gray eyes. Eyes that had seen awful things and were still trying to make sense of them, hoping maybe this would be the day that the man with all the answers would walk through those doors. "You fixing for revenge, I guess."

Trevor only returned the stare not wavering. It was enough.

"Dangerous game with a dangerous adversary. I've heard stories. I hope most of them lies or at least embellishments. Stories that will make you question reality, God, the devil, humanity and its capacity for depravity. To catch one like that, to take revenge on one as black as that, one has to do more than touch the darkness, one has to know it, become it. You won't ever be able to come back from that. You willing to become that?"

"She left a message for me saying something similar with the man you called Cyrus."

"Well then?"

"I'm here talking to you."

The priest grunted. "I won't pretend to understand what you went through. What you're going through. I've heard the tales enough times from people I knew, people I called friends and I saw how they changed. Saw that light leave their eyes."

"What I always wondered was if one were willing to go to any lengths to take their revenge on her, to kill her and end her reign of terror, would they be any better. Would any of us be? Would we suddenly wake from our comas and see the true light?"

Trevor shrugged, "Once you've seen what I've seen and felt what I've felt those questions become irrelevant. In fact, they never even crossed my mind."

The priest measured him with his eyes, he sensed the coldness, could feel that feral instinct that called for blood, that had become instinctual. Trevor was becoming a mechanism of hate, a force of destiny or maybe its tool. There was no reason to get in his way. Truth was, it was the only way to answer the question he had posed, someone needed to kill her if they were to see what happened at the end.

"There is a mutie that lives at the base of Blood Mountain. Some call him a shaman or a mystic warrior, whatever you want to call him, he's been given many titles that come with even more legends. He may know more."

Trevor wondered if this was part of the witch's trap. If she was sending him to the mountain, surely she would know of the existence of such a shaman. He had only heard of muties but never encountered one, at least as far as he knew. Some said they were deformed from the experiments that were run on them by the ancients, or they had been created by techno sorcery. Some said they looked very human but had longer life spans and could manipulate the darkta and illukta. He did not know the truth of any of these legends.

"He knows the ways and arts of the witch and mayhap can help you on your quest," the priest finished.

Trevor nodded, "Thank you."

"Don't thank me yet. There's a three-day walk between here and there. I'd take that time to think about what you are doing, ask if those you mourn would want this." He swallowed hard, "She is darkness my friend. She is a force of nature, the shadow to nature's light. Sublime and terrifying by turns. She will suck the light and life out of you no matter what the outcome and someday a man will walk through those doors," he paused to turn and point at the saloon doors with a crooked index finger, "and sit there much like you do now, angry, sad, full of hate, and say he's looking for a man, an evil dark soul that ruined his life, a man that looks exactly like you."

The silence between them stretched out, neither wanting to break the quiet. The bartender cleared his throat, made uncomfortable by the conversation and then this heavy silence that had settled on the air. Trevor raised his glass, the priest his. They clinked glassed and drained them. There were no parting words, what needed to be said had been said.

Chapter 4

The air was cold, his breath clouding in front of him, a thin layer of frost covering the thick blanket of dead leaves that crunched below his feat. The forest, dense with white birch trees, was menacing at night, offering a maze of thin white columns to navigate through and around. A bright full moon burned in a cloudless sky, the labyrinth of birches casting deep distinct shadows upon the frozen ground, forming a grid pattern of dark shadows. Eager to get to the base of Blood Mountain, he had chosen to continue his trek during the night, since the moon offered ample light to navigate by, but now he questioned the logic of that decision.

Growing up he had hunted with his father and spent many a night in the woods, and there was nothing unfamiliar about it. Even in adulthood he had spent many nights in the woods hiking to Hashen, Gilead, or other nearby towns for his blacksmithing supplies. But this was different. There was something alien here, an ominous, malicious presence hiding in the shadows, camouflaging itself in the maze of white striated bark, black earth, twisting roots, fallen leaves, and stirring shadows. He could sense it as the hairs on the back of his neck stood up, galvanized by the energy of whatever lurked in the deeper shadows.

The landscape was transformed into a chiaroscuro, the blue white light of the moon falling unevenly through the branches of the birch trees, creating a surreal landscape composed of stark contrasts. The oddness of the environment and the evil energy that clutched at his heart and whispered to him on the wind were harbingers of some apocalyptic or revelatory event. Every step echoed and reverberated in his ears, leaves crackled beneath his feet, the skins he wore scratched together as he walked, his breath ragged and rumbling. He was a blazing target of sound and shape in the forest. Mouth dry with fear, he reached out with his senses, attuned to every fleck of light, every pattern of shadow that appeared out of place.

There was motion to his left and he swung his head around, nothing. The trees sighed, creaking, shadows of branches lengthened and writhed like desperate grasping fingers clutching for purchase. There was a face protruding from the trunk of the tree in front of him, he jumped back and it disappeared. He leaned forward and he saw an eye protrude from the smooth white bark of the tree's trunk, the remaining features of the face cascading to the other trees, a patchwork face created from the maze of the multitude, mouths woven of rough bark, eyes flashing black, and white glinting blue in the reflected light of the moon. He could not breathe. A screech owl screamed in the darkness, startling him, forcing him to breath, as his vision began to collapse into a tunnel of unconsciousness. A mist began to roll in toward him from the west, swallowing the face by degrees, feature by feature, brows, eyes, nose, and mouth. Gone.

The mist came at him like a malevolent force, attacking him with a wall of cold and damp, icing his face, chilling his fevered flesh. He shivered as invisible cold daggers raked across his skin and icicle fingers enveloped him in a frigid embrace. Visibility was cut to an arm's length, the moon blazing in a haloed haze above as if seen from deep below the ocean, a hazy light of promise that he craved to ascend to so that he could breathe air again. He stopped moving, leaning over his knees, gasping for breath. He could not spend the night in this forest, he would die of fright, but he did not know how he was going to safely navigate his way out either. The screech owl screamed again, much closer this time, forcing another startled breath into his lungs. The owl's huge head appeared through the mist before him. It was the size of man's head, forming in fragments from the mist, its hooked beak emerging first, followed by golden eyes with dark pupils reflecting the blue of the moon. The head and neck were perched upon the downy, feathered body of a man— a barrel chest, a long torso, and an erection that poked toward him, large enough to be a horse's. It spread its wings out above him, the tips of its feathers touching above its head, a halo of plumage. It let out a blood-curdling screech, raising its head to the moon, and then immediately began to melt like a wax figure exposed to extreme heat, its beak and eyes running down its body, staring fixedly at him as they streamed down the midline of its torso. The upraised wings folded in, collapsing and melting into the body, legs shortened as they melted like wax candles to the ground and formed a gray pool that the creature began to sink into. Its erection poked from the ash-colored pool, standing upright like a marble monument, before going flaccid, the tip bending to join the pool in a waxy rainbow that shimmered in the moonlight before disappearing completely.

He dared not step in the pool that was blocking his path west, so he tried to move and sidestep around it. His plan was to run. Run west, out of the forest, out of the night as fast as he could regardless of what he encountered. Just keep moving, just keep running.

"Aye, you must be of stouter heart than this to play at this game." The words came from everywhere, he glanced all around him, head swiveling, eyes roving in their sockets, looking for a target but the mist was impenetrable.

"You said it would begin once I crossed the mountain!" Trevor screamed

She laughed, "This is not the beginning. This is mere taunt, an old witch's folly. From what I sees, you best turn back. Heart such as yours only good for breaking."

"Fuck you!"

"No steel in those words. Nothing but fear. And I eat fear. Go home and grieve your loss, grieve your fear, your incompetence. And die lying in your bed, a sad lonely nothing who lived a life of nothing," she jeered.

A naked form stepped from behind the closest tree. It broke his paralysis. He pulled his dagger from the scabbard on his hip, raised the blade to his shoulder, and struck at the form's chest with a powerful thrust. He felt the blade pierce flesh then hit bone. He was staring down at white milky skin that was all too familiar, a cluster of freckles creating a constellation he had gazed at many times. He raised his eyes to the collarbone that he had delighted in kissing, then to the hollow of her throat, and upward to gaze into the warm brown eyes of his wife. Her pale lips moved, "You don't have to do this Trevor. There is no guilt in letting it go, no shame in it. A true man, an honest man could go home and honor us in kindness and love."

He kissed her lips as she breathed her last, becoming smoke with a sigh, part of the infernal impenetrable mist.

"Damn you," he yelled as he whirled around searching for another target to use his dagger upon.

"Now there is some grit," she goaded.

The mist parted and before him was a path of rough flat stones, weaving slightly for about thirty feet to the bloodred door of a small hut. The building was made of various hues of stone covered in moss, thick milky windows stood to either side of the door, but he could not pierce their opacity and see what was beyond. There were no shadows, no flickers of motion.

This is where the witch came from. It was her dwelling. He could feel the weight of its dark magic and knew that although he could see it, it did not completely exist in the place he defined as reality. The dwelling was an island that existed between dimensions, existed in and between the dark spaces of the world, constructed of night and darkta energy. He moved closer, drawn by its power, his legs shuffling forward without any conscious direction, a force pulling at him. The various stones were finely etched with darkta spells and symbols. Black moss grew on the stones but would not grow over the etchings, making them more distinct. Symbols glowed in the blue-white light of the moon. Some of the stones were made of a material that looked like smoky onyx and amber-colored glass; they glowed with a dull light, forms swimming behind their surfaces, worms, snakes, and monster abortions floating lifelessly within the smoky glass. He was captivated by their glow and what skittered behind the surface, mesmerized. There were stones of silver and other metal and still others that reflected like a mirror, his face swimming and distorting in their surfaces. The wall was a patchwork of various materials, some natural, some maybe created by the ancients, and still others that were otherworldly, created by magic or stitched together from strands of the darkta.

The doorknob was cold as ice, his hand freezing to its metallic surface as he turned it. Darkta symbols swam across the door's liquid crimson surface like a school of fish, spiraling outward in one direction and then quickly turning and spiraling in the other direction, the spiral collapsing to a point before expanding outward again in a spellbinding pattern. He felt his mind tipping toward some new form of consciousness, a buzz filling his head, eyes blurring out of focus, yet the air had an edge that he could feel in the tingling of his skin and the twitching of his muscles, as if sensing the vibrations of subtle forces unseen.

He heard a deafening click as he turned the knob another degree and then pushed the door inward. Musty air filled with the smell of ancient things rushed outward, the seal of a crypt broken, spilling its hermetic secrets with the escaping air. A cacophony of ghostly voices whispered in his ear in a stream of language he could not interpret but which had the effect of turning his heart to stone.

As the whispers died on the air, he gazed into the room beyond. There was a small empty straw bed in one corner with a stained and threadbare sheet covering it. Everywhere else there were books, papyrus rolls, and magical bric-a-brac. A globe spun in its stand, detailing countries he had never seen the likes of on any of the maps he had studied in geography class when he was in school. There was a shelf with bottles containing powders and potions, and other larger vats that contained dead trophies, eyeballs, ears, penises, floating in yellow fluid; his nose detected a hint of formaldehyde. On one portion of the table he saw clear bottles filled with a transparent colorless liquid. Lying in front of them were syringes similar to those Trevor had seen at Doctor Talbot's house. But the doctor had kept them as antiques, the liquid sorcery they had delivered into skin and muscle long since gone with the ancients. Had the witch existed in the time of the ancients? Had she stored their magics in this hut to aid in her campaign of spreading sorrow? Is that what she had used to heal Jake, one of these needles filled with a liquid that would kill the dark poison in his body?

Trevor's eyes roved the interior, trying to take it all in, a dizzying array of objects heaped in piles or scattered over surfaces with no discernible order or purpose. And then a motion caught his eye, drawing his attention to the cold hearth directly across from him. It was so large and deep that its back wall was hidden in shadow, and as he stared he could have sworn he saw another doorway open. He started to pull the door shut, wanting to be away, feeling an immediate sense of dread, but there was also something pulling at him telling him he had to see. His body hidden halfway behind the closing front door, he watched in horror as a huge, dark, menacing form stepped halfway onto the hearth. He could hear its ragged breathing, its body seemed to expand with each breath, dark hair covering its body, yellow eyes glowed from the darkness, and he heard the wet smacking sound of a thick tongue running across sharp teeth. Trevor was sweating. The monster leaned forward slightly, the elongated nose of a wolf pushed past the darkness, sharp teeth gleamed from snarled lips.

He wanted to scream. His body felt frozen in place and he focused all of his energy on breaking the hypnotic spell and escaping. He fought to close the door; with each inch he regained more of his faculties, the hex beginning to break. With a final burst of willpower, he slammed the door and took a step back, expecting the creature to burst through and give chase. A heartbeat, a breath, nothing.

The sound of footsteps running up behind him forced him to turn his attention from the door to the woods. He searched the mist and turned three hundred and sixty degrees looking for their origin. The hut was gone, retreating back into the dark dimension that he had briefly glimpsed. The sound of a snapping branch rang through the forest and he turned again.

She stood there in a long robe woven of earth, root, and leaves, emerging from the trees as if birthed from the forest and mist, left eye bulging, pulling him, enchanting him. The air seemed to warp around her, folding and forming a tunnel that originated from her eye and ended at the base of his nose directly between his eyes. It forced his eyes to cross, the trees dipped toward the swirling cyclone, perfectly straight trunks suddenly bending in the middle as this dimensional warp pulled them down, bowing to the dark force of the witch. Shadows danced around the tree trunks, pulled into the gravitational spin, forming a black tornado. The pain in his skull increased, he felt exhausted, an icicle tip forced its way into his head, and he screamed.

His head leaned against a birch trunk, the tip of his knife buried in its bark. He could feel the heat of the sun at his back. He pulled his forehead away and touched the place where the icicle had probed him, expecting to find a hole, blood, but there was nothing. The mist had receded, tendrils hovered low at his ankles as the ground began to thaw. He put the knife back in its sheath and began to run away from the sun, heading west again. He did not, could not, spend another night in the forest. He would run all day if that was what it took to get away.

Muscles burning with acid, mouth and throat dry, he ran. Pain wracked every sense as his heart drummed, pumping blood through muscles that burned with every contraction. He had begun to cramp, his every breath seemed too shallow, his head swam, as he struggled for more oxygen. His world was pain, but the ghost of the witch chased him, spurring him on. To quit, to walk, would be to give in to her, would be to give in to pain and abandon his will to her. Whenever he glanced behind him, he saw her in that earthen, rotting robe standing next to her hut, waiting, one arm outstretched, palm up, talon-tipped index finger curling in a "come here" command. His heart would cramp and he would turn from the illusion, stare west, and run.

Beyond the pain he found a quiet place where everything was clear, the beauty beyond the torture. In this dimension his lungs inhaled air tinged with the smell of pine and cedar, his feet floated above a soft carpet of leaves, his eyes gazed upon a forest sparkling with light. His wife and son playfully hid behind trees giggling, his son took up the pace beside him, a look of pure joy on his face as the wind tossed his light brown hair behind him, brushing his cheeks with its cool fingers. They gazed at each other for a moment, a miraculous second that expanded to eternity. A tear fell from the corner of Trevor's eye, one born of joy, and it felt warm on his cheek. As he reached the end of the forest, his son's magic faded, as did the euphoria. As he entered the tall grasses of a valley meadow, he slowed his pace, feeling pain everywhere, his leg muscles burning and then locking up in a spasm.

Across the expanse of grass, maybe a mile or more to the west, was what he assumed was the base of Blood Mountain. His eyes moved upward over razor-sharp rocks to a dense line of pines that gradually diminished to rock again before turning to glacier and reaching the snow-capped summit. A stream ran from the glacier down the face of the mountain; its water was the color of blood. The sun blazed down upon the peak, suspended for a moment at its zenith, its rays transforming snow and ice to sparkling crystals, before it slowly ticked toward descent.

The mountain was huge, easily the highest peak he had ever seen let alone climbed. For some reason he had thought of the crossing as symbolic, he had not thought the ascent to be a challenge in itself. There were two things he now knew he needed to remember if he were to fight this fight: "Don't assume anything" and "Don't believe the witch. The witch lies."

He stood still, struggling to catch his breath, hoping the burning pain would drain from his muscles and the cramping would stop. He did not want to sit down, fearful he would be unable to get up again. The cold ground would not be a good bed. As he waited for the cramping to subside and his breath to return to normal, he scanned the valley and the woods at the base of the mountain. To the north there was a small hut made of stacked timber sealed with pitch, the front door faced east, smoke rising from the chimney at the west end of a severely pitched roof made to slough off the deep snows that would pile up and collapse beams with its winter weight. Although he had sworn off assumptions, he nevertheless had to assume this to be the dwelling of the shaman the priest had told him about, for there was no other human habitation in sight.

Further north and south were mountains stretching to the horizon in each direction. None as tall as Blood Mountain but none a mere hill to traverse either. Even if he were not to take the witch's bait, his only options would be to turn back east or follow the chain to the sea. To go west he would have to cross one mountain or another. But that was for later.

Using his long spear as a walking stick, he hobbled toward the hut, continuing to scan all directions for potential attack, for the previous night's fiasco had taught him a valuable lesson. Until this was over there would be no rest. He had to maintain discipline and could take nothing for granted. Not even what his eyes told him. He was open to pitfalls in every direction; every object, even his own thoughts, could become a means of attack.

Even with this new attitude and stretching his awareness to its limits, he did not detect the shaman. Slowly he made his way through the meadow, using his spear as a crutch, and then hobbled up the front steps to the narrow porch. He was about to knock on the door when he felt the muzzle of a gun pressed up against the base of his skull. He felt the cold steel pushing at his skull, a frigid circle that outlined the hollow bore that could spit lead death into his brain. There were a series of clicks as the hammer was pulled back, the cylinder turned, and then a final click as it lined a bullet up with hammer and bore, ready to fire. The sound was deafening in the silence, filling his entire awareness, there was nothing else but this circle of steel caressing his head and the death it prophesized. A shiver rattled down his spine and sent a frozen spike through the back of his brain, projecting the bullet's course. A deep voice rolled in like distant thunder.

"And who might you be?"

For a moment he could not speak. He tried to take a deep breath and was interrupted by the barrel being shoved more forcefully into his skull. "Well?"

"Nobody you'd know. Name's Trevor."

"And what brings you to my door, Trevor."

"The Coma Witch."

"She sent you?"

Trevor could hear the anger in the man's voice, the words spit from his mouth, teeth grinding.

"No! No. I'm chasing her. She killed my family."

"If you've met the witch, then you know there is no way I can believe you based purely on what you say. This could all be a lie meant to make me trust you and bring my guard down so that you can attack. Happened before. So what are we to do?"

Trevor had not considered this. He had been contemplating traps but had never considered the fact that he might be considered a snare for others sent from the witch. He had taken for granted that he would be believed. His pain and sadness had made him blind. He chided himself yet again, which depressed him all the more. The priest had been right, the man he was could not win this battle. He would have to become something else. But how? Defeated, frustrated, exasperated, he spoke, "I've come here to ask you to teach me how to find her and kill her. If you won't help me and don't believe me, then please just kill me."

It was not the words but their delivery and the pain than emanated from Trevor that convinced the man. He removed the gun. Trevor turned to face him. The shaman had high, jutting cheekbones, a long, narrow, jagged nose that had obviously been broken a few times, and long, straight, jet-black hair. A deep scar ran from the corner of his right eye down to his jaw line, a deep river of pain cut by some sharp blade. Above gray eyes was a brow that had the deep creases of worry and contemplation. Those stormy gray irises haloed the black sun of unwavering pupils that studied and examined him.

He seemed to come to a decision, blinked, place the revolver back in the holster at his hip, and then cleared his throat softly.

"I'll help you with a few conditions. One, you do what I ask without question. No matter how foolish or unbelievable it may seem."

"I shall."

"Two. You never give up. You kill her or she kills you. Those are the only two outcomes."

"Never quit till one of us is dead. Promise."

"Name is Rakesh." He held out his large calloused hand.

Trevor took it and shook.

Trevor looked down at the gun, somewhat in awe of it. His grandfather had had one, but only a handful of bullets. They had used it a few times to hunt deer, and then grandfather had told him he was saving the rest for a special occasion that, to Trevor's knowledge, never came. That was the only gun he had ever seen, and when his grandfather died he had not found the gun among the old man's belongings. As a blacksmith, Trevor believed he would have been capable of creating a gun but he had never found a reason for doing so. In Devon, there was no law against the use of ancient techknowledgy but there was a social more in place that said once an object of techknowledgy ran out or stopped working it was not to be repaired or recreated. Doing so could lead down the same slippery slope the ancients had found themselves sliding down.

"You seen one before haven't you?"

Trevor nodded.

"I only have a few bullets. Save them for the people that walk up to a door in the middle of nowhere and come knocking." He grinned and then gave Trevor a wink.

"Come in. One night's sleep and then we will begin your training tomorrow."

Trevor nodded.

Chapter 5

That night Trevor told his story to Rakesh, who listened intently and without comment. Trevor sat on a rocking chair next to the fireplace, with Rakesh sitting opposite him. The cabin was cozy despite the sparseness of furnishings. There was a wooden cot to the right of the fireplace with a quilt and a feather-stuffed pillow. To the left there was a sink. Skins hung on hooks or were tacked with nails to the walls—bear, deer, wolf—and on the wall closest to the door hung various tools—axes, knives, and other weapons. It was a room built with only utility in mind, the only items of luxury being the rocking chairs, which were very comfortable. The mere act of sitting and the mesmerizing rocking motion put him at ease and allowed the months of constant activity to drain away. For a moment he was transported back to a time before any of this had started, before the witch had come into his life, when life had been "normal."

When he was finished telling his story and how he had arrived at Rakesh's doorstep, Rakesh told him to go to sleep. "This may be the last night of good sleep you may ever have," he had whispered prophetically. After a pause Rakesh then added, "Tonight I will protect your sleeping mind. I will not allow her to enter your dreams or send you nightmares, but it will be the only time I will do it for you. After this you must learn to do that for yourself and suffer under the lash of her nightmares until you do." He scratched at his chin and then added, "First lesson: Pain is a powerful motivator. Darkness can lead to light."

He slept well that night under Rakesh's protection, but Rakesh had been correct, it was Trevor's last night of peaceful sleep.

The following night it was not nightmares that kept him awake but pain. Every bone, muscle, joint, and tendon ached. Every part of his body had either been sprained, pulled, bruised, beaten, tortured, or exhausted. He wished lesson one had been levitation, because there was no position that was comfortable, and every movement made in an attempt to find elusive comfort resulted in more pain. His body had become so attuned to and consumed by pain, the flexing of every muscle, the movement of every joint, the twitch of every nerve, transfixed his consciousness. He became aware of how gravity pulled on his skin, on his bones; when he laid down he was acutely aware of how its force pulled his body into the wood of the bed. He became aware of things he had never thought of before. Every hurt became a lesson of pain and an expansion of consciousness.

"Your body must become a nonissue. Decisions should be made without second guesses made by the body. The only way to train your mind to consider the needs of the body as irrelevant is to put it into a state of constant suffering. You then become aware of every cell of your body and are able to let it go through that awareness."

Trevor had not liked the sound of that. It was the first thing Rakesh had said upon waking him and pushing him outside into the cold air, followed quickly by the command: "Strip!"

The air was cold, his naked body steamed in the frigid air.

"See that rock there," Rakesh was pointing at a moss-covered, round granite stone that lay a few feet in front of him. "Carry it however you like and circumnavigate the entire meadow staying within the tree line." He gestured with his hands to encompass the entire expanse. Trevor guessed at a glance that it was a mile or more in circumference. When he picked up the rock he estimated that it weighed about sixty pounds. He hugged it to his chest; it rubbed abrasively against his skin, and in order to carry its weight, he had to pull it into his body, which collapsed his chest and lungs and left him struggling to breathe. His arms were shaking violently within a few seconds but he only thought of how painful it would be to drop it on his legs or toes or how difficult it would be to pick it up again. After a hundred yards the soles of his feet were cut and bleeding. His balls bounced unprotected against his legs. He felt ridiculous, humiliated, weak, and soft, as if every weakness he had ever had and struggled to hide was suddenly exposed and in the process of being flogged. His back hurt, his body trembled, but he kept on until he thought he could take no more and made to rest the rock on the ground.

Rakesh shouted from behind him, "If the rock touches the ground, that adds another lap around."

Trevor cursed under his breath, "Fucker," and then tried to figure out what he was going to do. If he did not shake blood back into his arms they would spasm and the rock would fall. If he did not allow his lungs to take in a full breath he was going to pass out from lack of oxygen and the rock would fall. Either way the rock would hit the ground and he would start at less than zero. He leaned forward and placed the rock between his legs letting the weight rest on his thighs careful to ensure that neither his penis or his balls ended up being crushed by the weight. He took in a deep breath and then began to shake out one arm but he had to bend deeper to balance the weight so that the rock would not tilt forward. Already his legs were beginning to shake. He shook the other arm quickly. He could feel the fingers on his left hand and that feeling of being lanced with pins and needles had returned to his right when he was forced to pull the rock back into his chest in order to relieve his legs of the weight. He grasped at the rock with all his might, his arms were numb, nerves pinched by the rock making them dead weight. Somehow his hands continued to hold on by some force beyond mental control. With each step he struggled, the roots attempting to trap his feet or make him slip, the loose stones littering the ground threatened to cut the soles of his feet or roll his ankle, and all the while the muscles in his back, shoulders, arms, and hands cried for relief, his lungs aching for a full breath, burning. His mouth went dry, his tongue became a thick piece of leather, rasping, lips cracking, his entire being begged for water, each breath threatening a cough or convulsion that he knew would lead him to dropping the rock. Nothing he did could relieve the pain. Relieving one area meant increasing pain in another. His mind constantly searched for a solution, hoping to find just one moment of comfort, one position that allowed for a brief rest, and even when it found none it would continue to search for answers. These mental gymnastics twirled in tighter and tighter circles, scanning and searching for a solution while adding mental torture to his physical pain.

He was sweating in the cold, the frigid wind freezing the droplets to his skin. He shuffled another forty or fifty yards before having to rest the rock on his thighs again, but each time he did this the effort to get the rock back to his chest and stand up did not offer the reward it had at first. So he started to count his steps, trying to increase the number of steps he took before he had to rest the rock on his thighs. He did not look at how far he had been or had to go. He stared at the ground and counted, nothing more, trying to increase his steps with each painful cycle of thigh to chest.

For a time he existed in utter agony, but as he pushed on he came to a place where he just moved to the mantra in his head. He did not concentrate on the pain or the effort, only on taking the next step. He had no idea how long it took (hours he would have guessed) to get back to where he had started, but he had made it without dropping the stone.

He thought he saw a slight smile of approval from Rakesh, but it disappeared quickly. "I want you to stand with your back against the tree, feet out in front of you and then squat down until your thighs are parallel to the ground." Trevor groaned just thinking about it. He placed his back, probably the only area of flesh not yet scraped raw, against the rough bark of the tree trunk. He then began to squat down. "Lower … lower," Rakesh urged. Trevor thought he was going to collapse and just slide down till his ass hit the ground. "There!" Rakesh commanded, "Stop!" Trevor's legs trembled with the effort, every muscle in his thighs screamed from the exertion. "Now hold that position." Rakesh picked up a stick and quickly sharpened one end to a point with his knife and then stuck the stick in the ground, point up, between Trevor's legs.

"Motivation," Rakesh said, staring into Trevor's face.

If Trevor were to ease the tension in his legs, the tip started to poke at his scrotum. If he fell, it would pierce it or go into his anus, or both. He kept his muscles locked. He tried to control them and he could feel the point poking up, brushing against delicate skin; he hoped his feet would not slip out from under him. And while his body fought against gravity and his mind fought against the pain, he was hit with a bucket of freezing water. He went into instant shock, gasping for breath, muscles going into spasm, the tip pushed into his anus and he pushed up but there was no more power, nothing left. He could relieve some of the pressure but could not free himself from the point. He fought to find that magical place he had found with the stone, attempting to tap into that strength that was beyond the body. He did not push so much as imagine he was weightless, that his body was as light as a feather and required no force to move. The pressure between his legs eased and finally released. He got control of his breathing. He closed his eyes fighting to maintain this control while also praying this would be over soon.

Dusk was upon him, the red fiery orb falling beyond the peak of Blood Mountain. Once the pink and purple hues of sunset gave way to gray, Rakesh removed the stick and Trevor immediately fell to the ground, his spent legs folding beneath him once the dreadful incentive was removed. Another bucket of icy water was thrown on him.

"Get in your bunk naked. You can have one glass of water first, nothing more."

Trevor crawled to the hut and retrieved the glass of water that Rakesh had left for him on the table, slurping it greedily while kneeling on the floor, still unable to stand, his muscles convulsing. The last drop gone, he climbed naked into the narrow wooden bed the thin straw mattress allowing him to feel every knot and twist of the wood that served as braces on the frame beneath it. The mattress itself was itchy, adding to his discomfort and he came to think of it as a further method of torture rather than comfort. The floor would have been a better choice, but he had no doubt that Rakesh would chastise him for changing location unless ordered to do so.

If he slept he did not realize it, and after what seemed like an eternity of pain, the sun rose in the east, poking through the bottom of the window, piercing his eyes with white-yellow rays of light.

The second day was so much worse than the first. More of the same exercises followed by runs up the glacial stream, climbs up cliffs of stone that held patches of ice and snow that froze his hands and feet till they felt like solid clubs hanging lifeless from his arms and legs. Then there were log carries, his shoulders covered in splinters and scratches from the rough bark. All of this accomplished without clothing, in the freezing cold, as his teeth chattered. The skin of his torso was in a constant state of confusion, going from sweaty to numb and then back again through a painful transition of pins and needles. No matter what he did, his limbs were just cold, barely controllable dead weight, no matter how much blood these exercises pumped into his muscles. He had never known such pain for such a length of time and had had no idea that it was possible to survive such an ordeal. Strangely, this torturous routine had a way of focusing him. Beyond the pain there was a new form of consciousness, there were moment of peace to be found within the torment, moments of clarity that went beyond the concerns of the body. Each new tribulation became an opportunity to explore this new dimension and expand it. His mind and his body became stronger.

That night as Trevor sat outside by the fire, shaking with cold and dizzy with pain, Rakesh told him about the purpose of pain in his training.

"When I was trained, my master told me that the ancients had athletes that could do incredible things. Their bodies had been modified by sorcery. I am a descendant of such athletes. My life span is longer and I have more strength and endurance than a normal man. It is why I am called a mutie. So I know by experience that their performance was enhanced by such modifications but what made them amazing was their ability to enter what my master called a 'flow state.' Whenever these athletes attempted some new feat, they were faced with the extreme consequences of failure and because of that their minds and bodies quickly adapted to new conditions by rewiring the correct nerves and cells, allowing them to perform such amazing acts of daring. The ability to manipulate their neuro and body chemistry in such a way became known as "flow hacking." Entering a flow state allowed their minds to transcend the apparent limitations of the body and reach a state where time slowed down, where they were one with all things and their focus was all encompassing."

"Is that what you are teaching me?"

"It is not something that can be taught exactly. It must be experienced. My goal is to put you in a state of pain, performing acts with dire consequences until your mind naturally finds that state. For instance, how do you feel?" Rakesh asked.

"Sore. Hurt."

"No. Become aware of how you feel and tell me in detail."

"I can feel my blood pulse against the walls of my veins as it travels around my body. It is a dull but insistent thud that hurts my head. My muscles quiver, the acid in them trying to escape through my skin, as the cells try to recover, nerve cells firing in the darkness of my brain telling my muscles to lock and spasm," Trevor replied.

"You see, you have already mapped out the territory. You understand what your body is going through. The flow state will allow you to use that awareness to push beyond and tell your body what to do, because it needs to do it in order to survive. At that point you will no longer be a slave to your anatomy. You will be its master."

"Those ancient athletes were as much mystics as anyone else. They were able to accomplish in months what mystics would spend years searching for in isolation at the top of a mountain. The monk had intent but no consequences for failure. It was the consequences, the pain, the threat of death that pushed these mystic athletes to their peak, allowing them to accomplish things that had been thought impossible only moments before. They had tapped into a resource beyond the physical and gave the ancients their first glimpse of deity. But on their way to making themselves gods, they forgot about humility, they forgot about the All and soon lost their way."

Trevor shrugged. At least now he was reassured that Rakesh was not just a sadist and that there was a purpose to the training, but that knowledge did not make him feel physically better. He let his head sag, his eyes closed as he searched for a place within that did not hurt. He was unsuccessful.

For the next month this daily routine of torture was his life. His mind learned every nerve, every reflex, and the process had triggered some hidden gift that lay dormant in the dark recesses of his brain. He found himself suddenly able to control that which he had always believed was beyond control. As pain made him aware of every nerve bundle, muscle, tendon, ligament, and organ, he found that once his mind had mapped these things with pain he could gain control of them at will. He could make them hurt with a thought or force them to contract or relax. He could convince his body that it was not cold, to cease its shivering, to not react to the pain that threatened to make his legs collapse beneath him, or to relax the muscles that made his hands clench in a convulsive fist. If he needed to determine how best to react, he could pay close attention to the pain and how it could be relieved but this became more of a clinical exercise, the true benefit was in allowing his mind to determine the best way for his body to respond to its environment in given situations and to conserve energy. When he could go all day and all night performing these physically torturous tasks, force his body to sleep and wake on command, then his training in the area of the physical was complete.

"In my clan there were warriors called the Ferah. My father was a Ferah as was his father. All the Ferah were descendants of muties. It was my heritage, and when I first came of age, I was initiated into the Ferah and was trained as one. The training was grueling, lasting many years, and was unrelenting during that time. It was a living hell. In one of the final cycles of tests I was climbing a rock face. My goal was to sneak up on the elders and overtake their camp. Three hundred feet from the ground I slipped and fell. I never remember being scared, something told me everything was going to be alright. Alain, one of my best friends, was climbing with me and watched me fall. He later told everyone that there had been something else with me, a spirit or black being that seemed to swallow me up as I fell toward the ground. But I never hit the earth; instead I was pulled into it, the darkta opening up as I slid through alternate dimensions disappearing into the earth. I couldn't see anything it was so dark. I thought for a moment that I'd been struck blind. Then all of sudden the symbols began to appear, burning in the darkness, they combined and unlocked further dimensions. I felt as if I were swimming in thick liquid like oil. Voices rose from the darkness. I could not understand what they spoke but it made me scared and elated at the same time."

"The symbols cleared, the voices went silent, and I was standing in the hollow of a dead tree. This particular tree was a holy tree that stood within the burial ground of our clan and was considered to be a portal to and from the underworld. When I walked out, our clan shaman was standing there holding his staff and glaring at me with fiery blue eyes. He pointed the tip of his staff at me, 'You took your time. I've been waiting here for hours.' Then he smiled, 'No more are you Ferah. I am your teacher now. Come.' And that was it. From then on I was trained as a shaman. Never would I be considered a part of the clan, even my family would not acknowledge me. In my clan the mystics and the shaman were separate. Revered but feared."

Trevor nodded as he listened with rapt attention, sensing the importance of what Rakesh was revealing.

"I will train your body in the way of the Ferah. They were clever and stealthy fighters but could also be fierce when the situation demanded it. The witch has many weapons. Some of which will be other people, animals, or monsters created out of darkta energy. She can control the minds of others, possess them, or merely have them do her bidding by holding a curse over their heads. She will use all at her disposal and you must be able to combat these foes. Against the witch herself these techniques will be useless. Only sorcery can fight sorcery. For that reason I will train your mind and spirit in the ways of the shaman."

Rakesh paused. Sensing that he was waiting for some form of acknowledgment, Trevor said, "I'm ready."

Rakesh flashed what Trevor called his sadistic grin, "Let's begin."

What Trevor had thus far completed had been nothing more than preamble. Rakesh had been punishing his body so that he could transcend it and now learn the utility of this newly sculpted tool. He was no longer the same man who had come knocking on Rakesh's door. His next series of lessons were in hand-to-hand combat. First he learned to use every hard surface of his body as an instrument to inflict pain on his opponent. Fist, elbow, knee, shin, foot, and even head were brought to bear as blunt instruments of destruction upon trees and branches. Push-ups were done on knuckles. Punching and kicking strength and speed were built up by performing a series of movement while submersed in the frigid pools of the glacial stream. When the edges of these pools began to freeze, he would walk across the ice to the black watery eye at the center, drop through, and proceed to crack and break the ice with his fists and feet.

When these movements had been mastered they moved on to rocks and sticks. "You may lose your knife in a fight or find yourself in a position where all you have is what is about you in the environment. Like the witch you must use everything you can to tip the balance in your favor." Rocks were thrown at trees, used to distract or cause long-distance damage followed up quickly with a running assault and a flurry or fists, knees, and elbows. Branches were plucked from trees and used as staves or swords to inflict damage at closer range. Using a leather strap he also lashed stones to the end of his makeshift staff to inflict heavier damage. Then he would use a curved staff loaded with a smaller stone. The stone would fly from the curved end as he brought his arm over his head in a throw. The stone launched from the staff became a deadly projectile flying at a speed faster than one thrown by hand. He became deadly accurate with all of these techniques and could hit an apple from a perch on a stump using any of them.

Through all of this training there was the constant sparring. Here Rakesh held nothing back. "You have to know how to react to full contact blows." The first few times Trevor was punched in the face or kicked in the gut or received a stick to the bridge of his nose he was struck dumb, and then Rakesh would attack in a flurry, swarming upon him. Then Trevor began to get used to it, the impact no longer upsetting his concentration or forcing him to retreat. In time he began to land some blows of his own.

Training moved on from sticks and rocks to blades, knives, daggers, swords, and spears. Trevor was cut, bloodied, pierced, and bludgeoned during these exercises. Even the wounds were a lesson, as Rakesh turned them into opportunities to show Trevor how to quickly stop bleeding with mud or moss and to treat the deeper, more persistent cuts with stitches or by cauterizing them with extreme heat. At times Rakesh injured him with the intention of teaching him more about healing, and he began to understand why he had been taught to listen to the pain and then dismiss it. He could heal himself with clinical precision because he did not have to fear the pain. He would not make decisions based on what would or would not offer the most pain. He would make the logical choice and would know its effectiveness by listening to his pain.

Rakesh promised that in the spring after the thaw he would show Trevor the herbs and plants that could be used to fight infection and relieve pain and itchiness, all of which were signs that the body needed further aid in healing. Without a store of his own herbs Trevor learned to use what the winter woods had to offer, brewing teas with willow bark to dull the pain from lacerations on his hands when it became too severe for him to dismiss and prevented him from gripping his weapons with the proper technique and force. In addition there were oils engineered from substances culled from the inner organs, brains, nerves, and muscles of fox, deer, squirrel, and bear that could heal cuts, bruises, and other skin lesions in a day.

They trained in the deep snow, the mountains and valley covered in four feet of powder. Here he was allowed clothes again. The mind could only prevent his skin from crystallizing for a time. Eventually all things were forced to bow to the will of nature and he was not at a point where he could will his body to not indulge in frostbite. He swam through the snow, digging for elms and maples to cut and carve for a bow and arrows; young maple saplings provided the most elasticity and strength for a long bow. He spent hours and days sitting on the porch with Rakesh, learning how to carve a bow and create straight arrows, and it was at these times that Rakesh would talk.

"These weapons will not kill the witch, nor will they work against the dark entities she conjures."

"For those there is only sorcery," Trevor remarked, remembering previous lessons.

"Aye. But there are different forms of sorcery. There are spells, incantations, potions, possession, astral travel, sigils, all of which you will learn, but you can fashion magical weapons that embody characteristics of other magical forms. This bow," he ran his hand along the smooth curved arm, "can be made magical in many ways. It could be fashioned from a magical object, be created through ritual, could be consecrated with magical oil, a potion, or have sigils etched into its surface, or any combination of these. This makes it a weapon of sorcery."

Trevor nodded.

"What you must learn is what magic to use for which weapon and which type of situation and adversary," Rakesh explained.

"And how will I know?"

"When you learn to read the darkness to see the magic all around you, you will know it in the same way that you would know to use a saw, not a hammer, to cut down a tree."

"And you will teach me how to see the world with those eyes?"

"That I cannot teach. I will teach you the techniques but their art is for you to discover. You can teach a painter how to hold a brush, how to mix color, how to shade, that is the science of a thing, but you can't teach him to be an artist, to see the world as only an artist can. That comes only with experience and a letting go of the belief that your eyes are the only way to experience the world. You must come to the realization that what you have been taught to believe to be true is in fact a lie. That there is light in the darkness and darkness in the light."

"My grandfather always used to say that darkness cannot exist in the presence of light."

"I've heard that sentiment as well. But what of the shadow that only exists because of light. Is that not a form of darkness?"

Trevor grunted, seeing Rakesh's point of view but not sure he agreed with it.

Rakesh continued, "Throughout all things runs the energy of darkta and illukta, one reveals the other. They are not in opposition, except in our minds and emotions. We feel the need to categorize, and once we do, we say one is bad and one is good. But what is light without darkness or vice versa? We are naturally drawn to a certain type of energy and to deny that is to live as a "normal"; one who decides not to decide, one who does not look below the surface. Mystics must be fearless, for they must accept what lies beneath even if it is ugly or scary. However, we grow up in society and are told to judge such things. The pessimist is told his attitude is wrong, the optimist that his is positive. Neither is true, this is simply a judgment."

"And you are saying that truth lies beyond judgment?"

"Yes. The truth is that the pessimist embodies more of the darkta and is naturally drawn to the shadow aspect of the self. When that person becomes a mystic he should be taught in the ways of the dark. If one were to attempt to train him in the ways of the light, the training would fail, because the teaching does not take into consideration the energy of the individual. This person may see that failure as a sign that he is not a mystic. But what has really been proven is that he was not a mystic who embodied illukta energy. This person may decide to simply be a "normal" and forgo any more training. To a darkta mystic the only way out is through. To deny the shadow is to deny the self and its place on the path to revelation."

"I am a darkta mystic as are you. We must accept that and move forward from that basis. And if we move through we can come to the realization of the illumika, the unifying force behind the darkta and illukta. It is the force that is beyond judgment, beyond the pairs of opposites. It is the sea in which the darkta and illukta swim."

Trevor could only nod, not completely understanding the concepts but feeling the truth of Rakesh's words in every fiber of his being.

Chapter 6

His sleep was tortured by nightmares. Some would start with pleasant memories as he would sneak up behind his wife and grab hold of her, arms enfolding her, kissing her cheek, he could smell woodsmoke and lavender in her hair, could feel it brushing softly against his skin, those brown soulful eyes staring up at him as she turned into his embrace. Suddenly that gaze would turn black and vacuous, devoid of life, black pits staring at him from her decapitated head on the table.

"Why Trevor? Why couldn't you do this one thing for us?"

"We could have been happy," Jake would add, his reanimated head next to hers.

"Appy!" Lydia would parrot in blissful incorrectness, and then a melancholy medley would ensue, the words swirling around him, echoing through his being. The scene would lose focus and swim, his family's disembodied eyes floating chaotically around him like large circular insects, finally coalescing into a single dark glassy orb that would stare at him from the ashy tumultuous sea of the witch's face, sneering lips pulled back in a knowing smile. He would wake sweating in his cold, uncomfortable bed.

Rakesh then showed him how to perform the banishing ritual before sleep that was effective whenever he was able to put his focus into the visualization of the symbols and sigils. On one of those occasions when he had performed the ritual correctly, he had had a sleep free of nightmares and realized upon waking that he missed them in an odd way. When he had them he at least felt connected to his anger, his purpose. When he banished the nightmares he found he had difficulty recalling his family's faces, their scent, and their smiles. When he became precise and practiced with the ritual, he only performed it on those nights when the training had been particularly cruel, so that he could get some restorative dreamless sleep. The other nights he allowed them to come, almost welcomed them.

Realizing that it was the darkness of nightmare that kept him connected to the memory of his family and his purpose in embarking on this quest, he began to think about the person he had been and questioned the person he was becoming. There was no denying that he was changing but he was not sure what he was changing into.

The snow had begun to recede, leaving only a thin layer of frosty white on the ground, marking the season when his mystical training began.

"Mystic lesson number one: Sorcery is not formula," Rakesh began. "What I teach you must become a part of you, and once integrated with your core being, it will change. If someone who is not an expert dancer watches a complex ballet, all they see is a dance made up of steps and motions, beautiful but not magical. But the dancer, with the eye of the initiated, sees the art, the grace, the intent of the motion, the emotion and energy. The dance then goes beyond beauty into something otherworldly, inexpressible. That is like the art of sorcery. It goes beyond the science of itself to become something more, the mundane transmuted to the mysterious."

Trevor had never been good at book learning. Memorizing a concordance of sigils and symbols for different objects, emotions, or actions was frustrating. Seeing this, Rakesh added physical training to the study. Trevor would be forced to repeat mantras that combined lists of symbols and what they represented. After picturing them in his mind he was to draw the symbols in the air, dirt, or water, all while practicing the martial arts in the cold springs, carrying the stone around the meadow, or holding himself up, knees bent as he squatted against the tree. And it worked. Soon the symbols seemed to arise automatically in his mind when needed. It was as though the physical demands had a way of loosening the tension in his mind to allow the symbols and their meanings to worm their way into the deeper layers of his consciousness. As he learned them he would practice further by incorporating the symbols into his everyday work, using them to represent some mental or emotional function or reaction.

"You then combine and overlay these symbols to create spells. All magic is about a focusing of the will on an object or objective. Your entire being must center on this objective consciously as well as subconsciously. Symbols are the language of the dark and deeper levels of consciousness."

Trevor continued to hone his skills and abilities day in and day out. The frost melted away in the spring sun, signaling that winter was finally over. As successful as he had been at learning the symbols and their purpose, he could not make the breakthrough that would take him from the techniques of magic to the art of magic. Where the magic became his. Where it was transformed and stamped with his unique magical DNA.

Seeing this, Rakesh had an idea. "I might have tried this with you earlier but couldn't during the winter because the correct ingredients must be fresh when synthesized. There are aids to shifting one's perception that we can employ in your training to help you make the transition from science to art."

"Aids? Drugs?" Trevor asked.

"A combination of plants and herbs that have the capacity of altering perception," Rakesh clarified.

They spent the next day foraging in the woods and at the base of Blood Mountain. They had gathered a blue flowering plant from the meadow, which Rakesh called meadow glory. The flower had five white oval petals, each with a blue stripe running down the center. When the petals opened to the sun, they revealed a small blue striated sphere the color of the sky. They harvested only the blue sphere carefully, cutting below it by feel with a small curved blade.

"The sphere will grow back. This does not harm the plant but it is only the first harvest of the spring that contains the psychoactive compounds we need," Rakesh explained.

Next were mushrooms with black caps covered with gray spots. "Only pick those that grow on the west side of the tree. Only the cap is psychoactive, but cut the stem where it meets the ground. This kills the plant, but the roots, the true nerve centers connecting all the mushrooms, will allow a new plant to emerge."

Rakesh demonstrated the delicate operation then turned the cap over. "These striations ..." he pointed with the tip of the blade at the gill-like structure on the underside of the cap, "contain spores in the deep folds. In the same general area where you harvested the mushroom clear away the leaves and needles to expose the black soil and then gently run the knife tip perpendicular to the gills, fanning them." Again he demonstrated. "This will deposit spores on the ground to replenish what was taken."

Trevor nodded took out his own blade and performed the task himself.

Rakesh nodded his approval as he watched Trevor fan the gills, depositing the gray spores across the black dirt. "Good. Two mushrooms are all we need."

After they collected three blue meadow glory spheres and two mushrooms, there were only two other ingredients needed. Both grew only in the higher elevations of Blood Mountain close to the tree line, where the rocks and roots were slick with a red moss, damp with the spray from the waterfalls of the glacial stream.

There were pockets of water where the red from the moss ran into the pools, coloring them bloodred. As the pools collected more water, they would slowly leak the colored water into the larger stream. The light cascading over the mountain deepened the color of the moss and the red of the stream, making it look like a river of blood.

"Blood Mountain," Trevor whispered, a grin forming on his lips. The first time he had seen the bloody stream he thought it had merely been a trick of the light. He had always imagined the name related to some horrid event resulting in a large death toll or was given in honor of some dark blood ritual that relied on human sacrifice. Instead it was due to the color of the moss and how it colored the water of the stream. Mundane. Banal.

Rakesh patted him on the shoulder, watching the spectacle himself, something he had seen many times but was always impressed with. "Sometimes the truth is so simple and much less mysterious and ominous than we think."

They both shared a smile as Rakesh knelt down. "We need to get the root. Pick a patch that overhangs a rock and roll it back to the place where its roots go into the soil. Roll it a little farther until you encounter some resistance but before you hear it tear. If you hear it tear, you've gone too far and damaged the moss. If that happens it cannot be harvested, you must move on to a new patch at least a foot or more away." Rakesh performed this task as he spoke softly, his fingers deftly rolling the moss back with a practiced grace. "Then cut along the underside of what you have exposed, close to the base while you gently pull. You should end up with a square patch roughly the size of your fist." Rakesh held the red bundle out to Trevor and gently placed it in his palm. "Your turn."

Trevor failed on his first two attempts. He slowly peeled back the moss, and when he felt the tension of the roots he would continue cautiously, but his fingers had not learned where the breaking point of the roots was until after he had experienced it the first time. The second time he had come closer to the pivotal moment. On the third try he was able to pause at the exact moment of tension and cut away the square patch he had exposed.

"Good," said Rakesh.   "We now take the blood water from one of these pools in a small gourd," which he produced from his satchel. "A mixture of all the ingredients will be brought to boil in the collected water."

The ingredients collected, they made their way back down toward the cabin. The sun spread its last rays of light over the top of the summit, before disappearing behind the peak, lighting and tracing the bloody stream and its branching tributaries down to the base of the mountain; they looked like the arteries of a massive giant, the moss, rocks, and soil transformed into its blistered multicolored skin. Rakesh and Trevor traversed the giant's torso, following its rushing arteries down the mountain. By the time they reached its legs the light was gone, the world cast in a uniform gray, muscle and skin transformed back into rock and root as darkness began to settle.

Back at the cabin Rakesh directed Trevor to create a fire within a copse of pine trees a few hundred yards away. Trevor made a fire within a ring of stones he had collected and formed beneath the canopy of pines. Under Rakesh's instruction he placed a tripod over the fire and hung an iron pot from the hook at its apex, its base hung a few inches from the licking flames. Rakesh poured the blood water into the pot. With that done they then turned their attention to the other ingredients as they waited for the water to come to a boil.

"The blue spheres need to be ground into a fine powder and although they are relatively soft, like a pea, you should always use a pestle or smooth river stone. The psychoactive compounds can be absorbed through your fingers or skin, so be careful not to let the powder get on your skin."

The three spheres rolled at the bottom of the wooden bowl. Trevor worked diligently to get them into a fine powder looking up at Rakesh occasionally to see whether he was doing anything wrong or whether the powder was fine enough. Eventually he glanced up and saw Rakesh nod, "Good. That is enough. Put the bowl aside for the time being.

"Next simply remove the caps from the stem. These will be placed on the top of the water as the other ingredients are brought to a boil."

"The moss will line the bottom of the pot. Lay it out flat, and as it becomes saturated it will sink to the bottom."

Trevor followed each of these instructions, glancing over at Rakesh after each step to ensure he had made no mistake. Each act met with a nod of approval and he moved on.

"Is the water boiling yet?" Rakesh asked.

"Yes."

"Remove the pot from the fire and place it on the ground."

Trevor did so.

"Make sure the blood moss lines the entire bottom. If not, use a stick or something else to adjust it."

Trevor made some minor adjustments with a stick lying next to the fire as Rakesh continued his instruction.

"Whatever pot you use you must always ensure that the moss lines the bottom. "

Rakesh leaned in to study Trevor's work. "Good."

"Now place the powder in the pot and, finally, place the mushroom caps peak up so that they float at the top and cover as much of the surface as possible."

Trevor obeyed.

"Good. Now place the pot back on the hook and let it boil."

Once the water was boiling again Trevor was told to count two thousand beats of his heart and then remove the pot. Rakesh put a wooden bowl on the ground and then covered the top with a concave screen of fine mesh. He glanced over at

Trevor to explain, "You can use cloth if you need to but you will lose some of the tincture and hence some of the power of the psychedelics to the fabric. Do not keep the fabric if you use it, poisons will be leached into it that can be absorbed by the skin. Just burn it but don't breathe in the smoke or stand over the fire as you do so."

Trevor poured the contents of the bowl slowly through the strainer. The solids sat at the top of the screen.

"Count fifty heart beats."

Trevor nodded at Rakesh when he finished the count. "Take another bowl or stone and push the contents gently against the screen, careful not to break the screen, and push the liquid through. This should even wring out any moisture from the moss and mushrooms. Then scrape the contents from the screen into the bowl."

Rakesh turned and glared at Trevor, making sure Trevor was attentive and listening. "The liquid is poison. Do not drink it. But you can save it in a sealed jar and use it to kill. It can be placed on weapons and dropped in food or drink. It brings on a horrible death—severe hallucinations, painful muscle cramps, and eventually heart attack. Most commit suicide before their heart fails, as they are driven to complete madness."

Trevor nodded and Rakesh moved on.

"Within the realm of the darkta this poison can also transform normal weapons into darkta weapons or increase their darkta energy retention. To understand that, you will have to experience it, but for now just understand that there are both a physical component of the poison and a mystical component that can only be understood when one is enveloped in shadow and directly experiencing the reality of darkta. In both realms the poison is dangerous and is to be used with care and clarity."

Rakesh continued to stare at Trevor, silently waiting for acknowledgment. Trevor finally nodded, "I understand."

"Now grind the solids into a paste with a stone then smear the contents over a flat piece of wood or a smooth stone and let it sit out in the sun all day tomorrow until it forms hardened crystals. As it begins to dry, place the crystals into a box or shield it from the wind, as the fine crystals will blow away if you don't."

Trevor listened intently to all the instructions. His head hurt from paying such close attention, but he saw that Rakesh was treating this with particular importance. There was the technique, the chemistry, the science, and of course, the warning that death or psychosis could result if the instructions were not followed carefully. But there was also the air of ritual and reverence and this seemed more important than even the overarching threat of death. The gathering of the ingredients and the awareness used to collect them, prepare them, cook them, and then grind them were as important as the actual technique. The ritual and the shift it created in his consciousness was as important as the technique.

"We are done for today. Keep the paste on the table inside the cabin for the night and place it outside in the sun come first light."

Chapter 7

They went to sleep soon afterward, both tired from the day's exertions. At first light Trevor placed the board outside, surrounding it with rocks to block the breeze. He then spent the rest of the day watching the concoction to make sure the sun was always on it. Throughout the day crystals began to form at the edges, a dull black-gray sand appearing as the water receded from the swamp of the tincture; the muck drying, hardening, and cracking as the water continue to diminish. He would scrape the ashy crystals from the shore of this diminishing pond and continued to do so until the black pool was gone. He then moved the dried crystals to a tin whose bottom was now covered with gray crystals that glistened red when the sun hit them, exposing the blood moss compounds hiding behind the gray.

That afternoon they returned to the copse of pine trees by the meadow facing one another across the fire. Rakesh had told Trevor to move the dried crystals into a small wooden box carved from acacia wood and covered in symbols and glyphs of enlightenment and revelation. On the hinged cover more symbols of magic were engraved.

"These symbols represent the layers of perception and reality from the depths of the animal Id to the height of the ethers where one can experience the perfection of deity in the plenitude." Rakesh explained pointing out the various symbols as he spoke.

Rakesh then went on to clarify the purpose of the ritual and the symbols. "Sorcery is about intent and will. Ironically, we must convince ourselves of what we want, for on the surface we can only guess. Deep down our shadows know. The purpose of ritual is to guide our intent to this deeper will and to make us consciously aware of it. Symbols and myth are the language of the shadow; consciously we may not understand, but the shadow reveals the meaning as it is exposed. The symbols then awaken that darkness within you that is then linked with the darkness of the All. It is not understanding that brings you to revelation but the transforming experience of dark and light energy, darkta and illukta. Study the symbols while you wait and align your intent with your dark hidden will. The ritual, in its entirety, is an act of sorcery that prepares your entire being for a shift of your consciousness into the dark dimension where revelation can occur."

In the hours before darkness Trevor studied the symbols, feeling calm and relaxed as his eyes traced each and every symbol, etching them in his memory. After a few hours of this, his eyes started to unconsciously rove the scarred landscape of the acacia box, the symbols blurring beneath his frenetic gaze; his eyes seemed to be ingesting the symbols, but what digested them went too deep to discern. Shadows lengthened and deepened as the gray of twilight became the darkness of night; the symbols disappeared in the darkness, burning only in the deeper darkness within his mind.

Rakesh returned as darkness began to settle in. He added wood to the fire and they began the ritual. Rakesh handed Trevor a pipe, "Take a pinch of the crystals and pack it in the bowl."

He waited while Trevor performed the operation. "Good. The compound can be ingested, but if it is you must take three times as much and you will also experience nausea and headaches; vomiting is very common. These side effects can obviously get in the way of the experience, so smoking is preferred. "

Trevor nodded. He continued to be aware of the import that Rakesh was giving to his words. This was a lesson that he might have been handing down exactly as it had been given to him, for his words and demeanor did not match his normal gruff tone. The scene was charged with ancient hermetic rites. It made Trevor both excited and scared. He had no idea what to expect. Life-altering revelations were not, in his experience, life affirming, and he was growing more and more concerned with what this awakened perception would show him.

"Before we begin …"

Trevor lay the pipe down gently in front of him.

"There are many dimensions to the universe and many reside in the shadows. There are multiple dimensions of thought, dream, psyche, the spirit; they are realities beyond normal comprehension and perception. The witch can manipulate the doors between these dimensions and bring objects, thoughts, and even emotions and experiences through one and into another. She can walk through the dimensional doorways of dreams and alter reality."

Trevor merely stared; his mouth had dried up; his tongue was thick and dead in his mouth.

"What is important for you to understand is that what you see is real, it is a shift of perception into multidimensional awareness, mystical, magical awareness. The drug will open your mystical eye here," he tapped the place above the bridge of his nose with his index finger. Trevor unconsciously parroted the act, remembering the icy dagger the witch had driven into him there during their encounter in the woods.

"This opening joins the physical sight with the higher and deeper levels of consciousness capable of perceiving these alternate dimensions. But it is not a hallucination. It is real and you must be on your guard."

"Can the witch travel physically through these doors?" Trevor asked.

"Ahh. You've seen it already haven't you? She visited you before. And till now you thought it was a hallucination but it was her. I'm sure she would have been happy to have you go on believing it was a hallucination or dream and hope you would just think you were going crazy. But it was real. You must stop trying to draw lines between the physical, soul, dream, and thought. They all exist on different levels of reality, each as real as the other, and at times they may even overlap and merge. To think that a thought does not have the reality and power of a punch is a fallacy."

"But how can she be in one place and then an instant later be somewhere miles away?"

"Everyone experiences it differently. Some have said that acts such as that are brought about by powerful magic that is capable of collapsing space, but I prefer the image of a dark hallway that travels behind all dimensions of reality, and in this hallway time does not exist. I can walk down the hall and enter different dimensions or I can take something from behind one door and then bring that object through another door. The hallway has no time, so I can move up the hall and perceive the future or go back down the hall and alter the past."

Trevor flinched, suddenly feeling a ghost of hope, "Change the past?"

"I know what you are thinking. You wonder whether you could you save your family?"

Trevor pictured them in his mind's eye, their faces took a moment to conjure, and when he did they were not as sharp as they had been, details were hazy. Would the time come when he would be unable to remember their faces? He nodded in answer to Rakesh's question.

"I won't say it's impossible but destiny has a way of correcting manipulations of such things. You change one thing and then the world shifts to correct it. The circumstances of their deaths may change but the outcome would most likely remain unchanged. The trick is changing small things that may modify perception or understanding but don't drastically alter the long-term outcome. Of course, these small trickles can have a cascading effect in the distant future."

Trevor's heart sank. But there was a chance wasn't there? Small as it might be.

"For tonight concentrate on the symbols and their meaning, and if your mystic eye is opened you can see how they are used to manipulate the dimensions and combined to create spells. You should also seek out what is called an aethenor, a multidimensional being capable of mapping out the dimensional doors. Shamans and members of my tribe used to call these spirit guides and in other cultures they were called angels, demons, phantoms, and ghosts. Their purpose is to help you find your way in the darkta and to teach you to travel through and in-between dimensions. It will enable you to experience the art of sorcery."

Rakesh paused to gaze searchingly into Trevor's face, "Are you ready?"

Trevor replied by picking up the pipe. He took a small burning twig from the fire and began to breathe in while he lit the crystals, the red in the crystals flashed deep crimson as they ignited. He drew in a long hard breath. The smoke was tasteless but there was a slight burning in his throat. He continued to draw breath until his lungs expanded to their maximum and could take in no more, then he held his breath. The crystals had disappeared completely from the pipe, lost to smoke. When he could hold his breath no longer, he exhaled slowly while staring into Rakesh's eyes. The dark pupils seemed to dance within the confines of the irises. It made Trevor dizzy to stare but he would not break the connection, feeling drawn into the dark oily pools, hypnotized as he was drawn closer. Time stopped and then suddenly Rakesh blinked, his lids falling slowly, heavily, blinds being slowly drawn across the window of his pupil, eclipsing Trevor's reflection, breaking the hypnotic state.

"You must do this alone. Choose a direction and walk until something tells you to stop. Your aethenor may reveal itself to you without you searching and it can guide you through the hallway of doors, and teach you the true mysteries of the darkta."

Trevor said nothing, he simply got up and left the warmth and safety of the fire, crossed the meadow to the east, and entered the forest. The moon was shining down upon him from above beginning its decent toward the west, his shadow slithered on the frosted grass as he neared the forest's edge. The shadows all around him had begun to dance, the branches bending and folding, becoming arms and hands that reached out for him, caressing his dark reflection with their spectral touch.

His head swam, his stomach tightened, and he felt warmth rising from the pit of his stomach up to his chest, filling his torso and then expanding outward to his legs and arms, tingling. The blue-white reflected light of the moon instantly became brighter and other colors began to form within it, creating patterns of symbols. The world shifted in front of him and he felt that icy dagger probe at the place between his eyes. He blinked.

When he opened his eyes the witch was staring back at him from only two feet away.

"Yous think your clever donst you, aye?" her voice beckoned, the sound of a deep horn, distant rolling thunder, echoing, reverberating, scarring the air with black waves of hate.

Trevor stood motionless but felt the pull of that dark bloated eye. God, how he wanted to stab the tip of his dagger into that black gelatinous mass, hear it pop and stare at the oily black contents oozing down her face as she screamed or dig it from her orbit and take it as a trophy.

"And what would you do with it then, aye?" she cackled.

Had he spoken aloud?

"I should just kill you now and end this game." She began to make a motion with her hands, a twirling of her arms about her head followed by a clenching of her fist. He felt a tightness in his chest. Again. Tighter.

Studying the signs and symbols that swarmed about him he struggled to pick out the patterns that could be combined to form a spell of protection. Finding what he was searching for he folded his fingers and hands, creating a symbol with them, while vibrating the words deep in his throat. The tension in his chest eased and the witch recognized at once what was happening. She pulled back allowing the spell to drop, deciding further effort was pointless.

"You might be fun to play with after all."

Trevor did not allow her to recover and launch another attack. He used a banishing spell to close the dimensional doorway she had opened. Immediately, she disappeared from view; a black silhouette marked her presence for a moment before becoming smoke, whisked away by the night. A red-yellow flickering light arose where she had been, growing brighter. A creature maybe two feet tall with a human form stepped into view slowly as if appearing from behind a hidden curtain. Its entire body was flame and light. When it moved, it looked like a candle flame blowing in the wind, dark eyes staring at him from the amber flames.

Was this his aethenor or hers?

"Yourrrrssss," it hissed into his thoughts. It gestured with its flaming hands for him to kneel.

Trevor looked into its black eyes, the only feature to emerge from the immolation. He stared into a reflection of himself, mesmerized. The aethenor raised its arm and touched the place at the bridge of his nose.

It was not the icy dagger the witch had used but was instead a flash of white searing heat that burned inward and set alight nerves and cells that had until then lain dormant. Trevor felt the flames lick at his senses, expanding and opening new perceptions. When he opened his eyes it was as though his vision were suddenly more complete. There was a thickness to the atmosphere and he could feel the air molecules smashing against his skin.

The aethenor then reached out its arm and pulled at something invisible hanging in the air; once it had a firm grip, it twisted its hand as though turning a knob. It then pulled at the invisible door and swung it outward stepping to one side as it did so. There was a rectangular space where the darkness was different, deeper. The aethenor pulled a symbol from the dark rectangle of the door and merged it with a symbol forming at its feet. Once the symbols were joined, a curtain fell over the world.

Trevor was staring at the accusing faces on the dinner table. The aethenor gently touched the top of each of the three heads and then danced over to the fire in the hearth and pulled a symbol to join it with another, and the black curtain fell again. The aethenor was bending its arms and waving its hands toward its face as if beckoning something toward it. Suddenly there was a rush of rectangles, a series of them flew past in quick succession. Trevor could only guess that this was the hallway of dimensional doors. As they flew by, the aethenor would put up its hand in a halting gesture to slow down or stop their progress. It would then open a door enough to let Trevor peek into the alien world beyond. Trevor saw a gray world that felt cold and smelled of rot, a world devoid of life. "Deattthhhh," the aethenor whispered in his mind. It slammed the door and moved on, opening other doors for short periods of time seemingly at random: a black void gaped, a world of fiery white light exploded, alien landscapes he hoped he would one day get to travel in and others he prayed he would never encounter again.

"Yooouuu." The aethenor was pointing at him, waving its arms, telling him to mimic the motion. He did. The doors moved by easily, as though he were swimming in a warm ocean current, moving in whatever direction he willed. It felt as though the world moved at his command. He opened a few doors; pilfering a symbol from one dimension, he would open another door, take another symbol, and then marry the two. It created objects and entities he had no words to describe. They were not objects in the physical sense of the word. They were ideas and concepts that had gravity and were real in a new sense of the word. Everything here required a new definition, a new understanding.

Once his mystic eye was opened it could not be closed. As Rakesh had once warned him, there were certain things he would see that could not be unseen and would change the way he perceived the world forever. This was one of those things. Everywhere he looked he could see the overlay of symbols and energy and the ability to manipulate them became automatic, because the symbols now made sense and their pairing was obvious, pieces of a puzzle that were made to be joined. All that was needed was a subtle manipulation, a shape rotated here and joined there placing the energies in the proper position to create a whole. Many symbols would tie together the molecular or even subatomic particles of matter that he could now see, understand, and control. This was the marriage of science and art; now he was the quantum mystic, capable of strumming at the threads that made up the instrument that sang the song of reality.

He played this harp for some time, finding such joy in this newfound ability, like a child given a new toy. Mixing symbols, creating patterns, feeling the energy that vibrated through and from all things, redirecting and bending those shapes into new patterns created a growing euphoria in him. Grass shook off its frost, trees bent to caress his head with the long gnarled fingers of their branches, and he felt like a god. He caused flowers to open and expose their solar petals to the lunar goddess, taking particular satisfaction in the paradoxical nature of his conjuring, exposing objects of the day to the night, with each revealing its secrets to the other.

As he played with these new abilities he came to realize that he could vanish into shadow and could squirm through the empty space of whirling matter. He could pass through the bark of a tree and enter its core, seep into the soil, become dissolved in the liquid of a stream. He could become one with the things he entered and then spread himself out into other objects, stretching outward to become a plenitude. He became transmuted into multiple drops of water, his consciousness spread out across the babbling stream, stretched miles long, experiencing every particle contained within it simultaneously, a liquid giant. The water would flow over rock, moss, and root, and he would enter it and it would become a part of him. He infused and became infused by all things, losing himself in the energy of the One and All.

The darkness cleared, the swarming dimensions halted and he found himself on the bank of the brook, the aethenor staring at him with those black eyes, its expression unreadable. It gave Trevor a comical thumbs-up gesture, twirled around on the toes of its feet until it was spinning like a top, flames stretching and forming a cyclone that thinned to an ethereal thread and then was gone. He was alone in the forest, the sun rising in the east. The light was warm, flashing yellow, orange, purple, and pink. Billowy clouds transformed into a canvas of color. Beautiful. He could still see it all, the complexity, the darkta and illukta, the chaos and ecstatic splendor of their opposing dance, annihilating each other as they merged, releasing new forms of energy that would then begin the dance all over again. At that moment Trevor knew he had been changed by the ritual of the mystic eye; he could feel it in every particle of his body. He had become an artist.

Chapter 8

"Now that you can see the darkta and have experienced it there is little more I can teach you," Rakesh said when Trevor returned from his night of revelation. The change was written within the fiber of Trevor's being, burning darkly in the early morning light and easily detectable to another of power like Rakesh. "But there is one more story I need to tell. Rest and we will talk tomorrow."

Trevor nodded and went into the hut and quickly fell asleep.

When Trevor woke to the sound of birds chirping outside, the soft morning light cascading through the high window, he expected the mystic vision to be gone. It was just a drug-induced experience, a dream, he told himself. But when he tried to conjure the symbols, spells, and dimensional portals of the darkta, he found he could do so with ease. Everywhere he gazed he saw the symbols of energy both dark and light, and if he concentrated he could go deeper and see the small particles that made up that energy, which he could also manipulate into spells.

He got out of bed, his body tingling with energy. There was no weariness; in fact he felt more awake than he ever had. He took in a deep breath, and with his new perception he could feel that space between his eyes open and expand and grow warm, energy pouring into him. Walking outside he gazed upon the world with changed perception. The world seemed hyperreal. The grass, the trees, the birds, everything was suddenly more vibrant, more present. Words could not adequately express what he perceived or the feelings and thoughts that overwhelmed him. To attempt to convey such experiences in words would be futile and result only in frustration.

Rakesh was approaching him from the forest and Trevor detected a warm orange glow surrounding him, acting as thin layer of light that protected him like a shell. When he reached out to shake Trevor's hand, Trevor could sense Rakesh's energy expanding and mingling with his own. He noticed that his own colors were gray-blue, fading to black closest to the skin. As they shook hands he watched an orange bolt run through his aura; the blue pulsed and a similar flash of blue made the circuit of Rakesh's aura.

"You see now." It was not a question.

Rakesh continued, "At the base layer life is energy and each discrete unit of energy, quanta, can be manipulated, combined, expanded. But it never disappears. It can take on a new form, or become temporarily invisible, but it is never destroyed. This is the powerful knowledge of the quantum mystic."

"Then there is no bad? There is only energy and quanta. You can't judge the right or wrong of a particle. It simply is what is. Right?"

"That is one view."

"And your view?"

"There are qualities and colors of quanta. We call the primary qualities darkta and illukta. Some mystics are expert in the ways of the light and others in the way of the dark. But to manipulate reality and hide the light or the dark and its energy is to disrupt spiritual progress, it is to become an illusionist whose only goal is to hide the truth. Our goal as quantum mystics should be to reveal that energy to others, to share it, to increase it. To manipulate for personal egotistical reasons, like revenge ..." he paused glaring at Trevor, making his point obvious, "is sorcery. The dark side of that power is tied to the individual ego and its wants and desires. It is not focused on the increase and expansion of the energy of deity. It is the illumika that unifies all forces, that connects all things and makes sense of them."

"Is that what the witch does, manipulate and hide?"

"Yes. She turns others toward the darkness, revealing only the despair and pain aspects of the darkta. She has manipulated reality to increase her perception of it, not the truth of it."

"And that is why she must die."

Rakesh shrugged his shoulders, noncommittal. "Let me show you something."

He turned and began walking up the mountain, following the blood-colored stream until he neared the tree line and then turned south to a small glade of trees. Within that patch of trees was a graveyard. A stick the width and length of a forearm was placed behind each mound, with a name and symbol carved into each smooth surface: Samuel, Earl, Ravi, Maria ... There were at least ten; he did not count or try to read all the names. He stared at Rakesh, confused.

"These are the graves of depraved souls that the witch sent to kill me. Do you know why?"

Trevor shook his head. His blood chilled in his veins.

"Because I refused to chase her."

Trevor swallowed. He was still confused. "Why did you chase her to begin with? What did she do?"

"That is the story I must share with you." Rakesh sat down on the trunk of a fallen tree on the outskirts of the cemetery. Trevor joined him.

"When I became a shaman I was isolated. After my training I never anticipated that I would ever have a family. In my tribe there was no rule that a shaman must be celibate or that he could not or should not have a family. But the rigors of a mystic life do not often align with the rigors and sacrifices of family life. For that reason most shaman are loners, observers on the fringe of society, called upon only to perform specific functions and tasks necessary to their tribes but at the same time always existing outside of it."

"Then one day I was walking through the woods and came across the body of a beautiful woman who appeared to be sleeping. I could easily tell from her features that she was not of my tribe. She had just been walking through the woods and was bitten by a poisonous spider that caused her airway to close up and she died of asphyxiation. She was young, beautiful, and I thought … what a shame. What a shame that she would never love another, never have children, never grow old and share her wisdom and her beauty and her love with others. All because of a spider. It made me mad and then it made me sad. So sad that I decided to do something I was told by my teacher never to do, I manipulated the darkta and created a spell of healing and resurrection that brought her back to life."

Rakesh paused there, the anger and sadness he had felt distorting and twisting his features, eyes becoming slits, mouth turned downward, reliving the events as he shared them.

"I'll never forget how she looked at me when she took her first breath. It was as though she knew she had died and was gazing up at a heavenly being. Her old life and the world she had lived in was no more. This was a new life, this was heaven. And that is how we lived. For me she had no past. Our history started at that moment and proceeded from that moment, that moment when she gazed at me through those beautiful coffee-colored eyes and gratefully made me her slave. We lived together in paradise and had a daughter that was even more beautiful than her mother."

"I had manipulated the darkta for personal reasons. And worse I had changed the will and history of another in a large way. And as I had been warned, the universe had a way of correcting such blatant, self-centered manipulations. Its corrections are cruel and this one came in the form of one of the witch's minions."

Rakesh forced a hard swallow, his eyes grew moist. His glassy stare was directed toward the forest but he saw only inward to the events in his memory.

"I had gone to town to perform a healing on a young boy and when I returned to our home I could feel the darkness. Something had been twisted and broken. I could smell the evil of it in the air. I ran to the front door and flung it open. On the floor rolled up in a ball was my beautiful wife covered in blood. From a gap in the crook of her arm was the face of our two-year-old daughter, eyes of slate stonily glaring at me, blank and lifeless. I can't even tell you how I felt. When I think back on it now I can only feel the sadness but at the time there was only disbelief and rage burning through me. What I saw didn't seem like it could be real."

A tear fell from the corner of his left eye. He did not brush it away but let it burn a line to the corner of his mouth.

"The blood was so thick that I didn't know what had happened at first but as I approached I saw the deep wounds, the slashes and puncture wounds created by a blade. My wife had curled her body around our daughter hoping to protect her. But the blade had been very long and the assailant had stabbed the child through her mother. I couldn't imagine the pain, the anguish, the fear. All of this collected in me. As a shaman I was trained to be empathic in order to heal and that training kicked in even though I wished it hadn't. I could feel the fear, the absolute terror she felt, hoping beyond hope that her body could shield the child and the utter despair when the child began to scream, knowing that her daughter was going to die, that her little Megan was going to die in pain and fear. There was a flash of anger. Where was he? Why was he not here to protect them as he'd always said he would be? The pain ended, replaced by gratitude when the blackness of death embraced her like a lover, taking all the pain and sorrow away."

He put his head in his hands reliving the moment in his memory, seeing it all as though it had just happened. "And in the deathly silence that followed I heard motion behind me and there in the corner was a middle-aged man, covered in blood, shaking, a long dagger clutched in his hands, knuckles whitening under the force of his grip. When he opened his mouth it was not his voice that came forth. 'Aye, cully. First your family and then your tribe. And once their alls dead I'll torture their souls in the shadow realm' She would not have had to goad me; I would have chased her anyway. Then there was that awful laugh and then the man's lids blinked over his eyes and he stood there as if not knowing how he'd arrived. But I knew. I knew there had been a deal. She had not possessed him during the act. She had made him a deal and he had taken it. I could see it in his conflicted eyes, he knew what he had done, had chosen it. I knew of the Coma Witch and knew she dealt in curses and undelivered promises. What she wanted with me I didn't know, still don't know. I think when I manipulated the darkta to resurrect Mona I exposed myself in the darkta and she became aware of me. She became the hand of cruel fate, setting destiny back on its proper path. Knowing all this there was a part of me that searched for forgiveness for this cursed man forced to make deal with her but only for a moment and then I didn't care about the why of it. That rage returned and without even thinking I attacked him, pulling the knife from his hands, kicking, punching, stabbing." Rakesh's hands jabbed and convulsed, as he relived the event, the phantom dagger clutched in his fist, knuckles whitening, eyes gazing inward to the past.

"I was covered in blood, breathing heavy. I was like an animal completely driven by hate and the instinct to kill. When I was done what lay on the floor barely looked human.

"And that is when I cried. Cried for Mona and Megan, for what I had done to the man and for what I would become in order to kill the witch. I cried for days, caught in some state where I was neither alive nor dead; all I felt was sorrow. I buried the only woman I had or would ever love and the blessed daughter she had gifted me with. Then I headed west following the shadow of the witch. She placed others in my path and I killed them as well. Nothing was going to stop me."

Trevor sat in silence, amazed at the similarity of their stories, the events in his memory juxtaposed, swam, and intertwined with the images described by Rakesh.

"And then when I got here to Blood Mountain, I paused. I don't know why, but I made the mystic crystals the way my teacher had taught me when I first became his apprentice and smoked them. It was then that I had my revelation and that I understood that I was becoming like the witch. I was killing innocents, I was killing those she had afflicted and twisted, regardless of who they were or what they had done. I had ceased to even question it. I was doing exactly what she wanted me to do. Unwittingly I had made a deal with her for my soul. To chase her, to kill her, would only increase the chaos and darkness of the world, and in my doing so she would win. The darkness would take my soul. Mona and Megan wouldn't have wanted that for me. To lose myself in order to kill her would dishonor their memory."

He glanced across at the graves and sighed. "So I remained here and she sent these people who she'd made deals with to prod me into chasing her. After Maria there," he pointed to the furthermost grave on the left, "she stopped."

Rakesh removed his shirt and on his shoulders and chest were symbols writ in some yellowish orange ink. "I removed the essential fluids and oils from their bodies and tattooed their symbols into my skin in the hope that my redemption would bring about theirs. That they can live in my flesh and experience the glorious redeeming energy of the illumika once I've transcended the darkta."

Trevor was staring, "But you told me that I must kill her."

"Or die."

"Yes."

Rakesh took a deep breath. "What if you could take in her energy or soul and redeem that dark energy in her? Prevent the collapse into darkness and instead expand into illumika, exploding creative light into the universe?"

Trevor was shaking his head, "No, don't ask me to do that."

"Revenge is black. Death brings about only more death."

Trevor did not have to contemplate his response, "I would die before redeeming her."

Rakesh was shaking his head. "This ultimately has nothing to do with her or with you. Think of her as a force of nature, a deity whose time for transformation has come and you the catalyst and agent of that transfiguration."

Trevor pictured his wife's eyes, felt her soft lips, hands raking through her silky black hair. Through clenched teeth he said, "If you have nothing more to teach me I believe it is time I cross the mountain."

Rakesh nodded. "Your pack is on the porch. I packed your personal belongings, some food, and various and sundry other items. I put one of the ancients' lighting torches in there to help start fires, but use it sparingly; it is on its last legs. Good luck on your journey. I wish you well. I wish us all well."

Trevor was still shaking inside but there was no doubt this man had saved him, had armed him with the only tools capable of killing the witch. He reached out his hand and Rakesh took it.

"Only light can banish the dark, Trevor. A shadow can only add to the darkness or be swallowed by it. Be careful which path you choose."

Trevor nodded, not fully understanding. He pulled his hand away, walked to the porch and collected his pack, and began the climb up Blood Mountain.

Chapter 9

Trevor followed the blood stream up the mountain, knowing that the stream's source was the glacier close to the peak of the mountain. The climb was difficult and he knew that had he attempted it six months prior, without training, there would have been little chance of his reaching the peak. As it was his breathing became ragged the higher he went, as the air thinned, forcing him to breath more heavily.

By sunset he was entering the cedar forest. The trees, stunted by altitude, did not reach more than twenty or thirty feet, but the shade gave him respite from the sun, which had started to shine directly in his eyes as it crested the peak and descended to the west. He was physically exhausted; his legs shaking like rubber and cramping whenever he straightened them. He leaned against a tree, his legs out in front of him to relieve the cramping and soreness. Touching the darkta or entering the flow state would have enabled him to continue on, but he listened to the needs of his body. His mind could only overcome certain forms of exhaustion and he did not want to overextend his body, knowing that the witch or her minions could strike at any time. When the cramps ceased, he took a few deep breaths and was asleep.

His eyes popped open. He had heard a crack, a branch breaking. Head swiveling, pupils dilating, he searched the dark for the source. He had not performed the banishing ritual before falling asleep as he knew he should have. In his exhaustion he had not even thought about it or the consequences of not doing so, but now he was acutely aware of his oversight. As he glanced around he began to wonder if this was a simple dream taking place in his head behind closed eyes or was the Coma Witch currently sliding through the dark spaces, her fingers inches from his neck. How would he know? Rakesh had warned him—all levels of reality had equal import at the level of darkta.

His eyes were suddenly drawn toward the tree trunk directly across from him. His right eye was pulled to the spot painfully, as though ethereal fingers were probing and squeezing it, first directing his vision but then growing more insistent as though attempting to pluck his eye from its socket. His vision focused on a knot protruding from the surface of the bark, and as he stared at it, an eye opened in the center of the knot staring back at him. Directly below the cyclopean eye appeared a nose and then a mouth, grinning toothlessly. The bark of its face twisted as it gawked with genuine surprise at finding someone to stare at.

"Trevor, I presume?" A rough reedy whisper, that combined the whistle of the wind and the creaking of ancient branches.

Trevor tried to open his mystic eye but the pressure in his right eye made it difficult for him to concentrate his energy in order to see the darkta. He still was not sure if this was just a normal dream or one guided by the presence of the witch. *Focus damn it!* he yelled inwardly. Was she blocking him from the darkta?

As if in answer the tree face spoke, "Sorry about this, couldn't be helped. Even we tree spirits are powerless against such things." Its mouth gaped and from this huge wooden maw a dark creature spilled like a fetus from a vagina. Its gray flesh was slick with thick mucus, shimmering in starlight. It looked half-baked, an alien face pushing out from the fetal ball, black eyes staring at him. He fought against his paralysis, the black gaze transfixing him, its skin smoking in the cold night, the sheen of mucus glistening in the starlight.

He reached for the blade at his hip just as the demon uncoiled. Its long, thin, bony body began snapping, as though its bones were reconfiguring, forming and locking into place. The shape of its head was phallic, the two eyes at the side of its face were angled forward floating on its skin, the slit at the tip of its head expanded, opening vertically into a huge maw rimmed with razor-sharp teeth. It lurched forward and he instinctively lunged outward with the knife, the blade searching for a slithering eye. The black orb erupted as the tip of the blade found its mark. Black ooze ran down its face. It put up a hand to protect itself but now Trevor had gained the moment he needed. The demon's attack had shattered his paralysis. His mystic eye opened and he found the darkta symbols and combined them. Part of its face was pulled into a hole in the dimensions he had created and then he quickly closed it. Head separated from neck as the portal between two worlds closed, eerily silent; the head disappeared into the void, the body fell to the ground at Trevor's feet, twitching once, twice, and then going limp, steaming in the cold of the night.

Before him, smiling from within the gaping mouth of the tree spirit was the witch. The large left eye, huge, a swirling vortex of darkness, pulled at his right eye painfully until the pressure became excruciating and he screamed, "You said after I crossed the mountain."

"Aye. So I did. But if you're not having fun now I don't expect it will get much better for ye." She cackled again, but the pressure was decreasing and the mouth was closing as she pulled back. The treeclops was staring at him again.

"There is some darkness men should never pursue. Sorry for you." With that the tree spirit closed its mouth, its eye winked shut, and the face was gone. He was left with only the knot, the darkness, the cold, and his fear.

Trevor awoke to the first rays of the sun, glancing to left and right searching for and expecting attack. Nothing. He brushed himself off as he got up, drank from the water bottle in his sack, and then made his way back to the stream, where he doused his face with water hoping it would help revive him. Before heading out he filled the water bottle again and began his trek through the woods toward the glacier and the summit.

There was an ominous feel to the air. He felt as though he was marked as a target, a black sun shining a focused ray directly on him, channeling every bad thing in his direction. It filled him with dread. When, a few moments later, he heard the howling of a wolf he knew it was hunting him. From here on out everything would be coming to attack him. She had turned all against him, finding that dark seed in each and every thing and turning it to her will. Her will was to punish him, torture him, and turn him into something evil, and the whole world—seen and unseen— was her tool. He pulled his knife from its sheath and hefted his spear, preparing for violence.

There was more than one attacker. The scurrying of multiple pairs of feet echoed all around him. As they got closer the pack began to fan out and circle him. He made his way quickly toward the stream hoping at least that if he put that at his back he would cut down their angles of attack. His blood was boiling in his veins, his heart hammering in his ears, his body pumping adrenaline.

He attempted to conjure the symbols but the fear had him and he could come up with nothing but a jumble of meaninglessness. A large black wolf blocked his path to the stream. Behind it was a rock shelf with the stream trickling down its surface, creating a bloody waterfall. If he could get past this one beast the ledge would offer protection from a rear attack. The wolf seemed to sense his intent, blocking his path to safety but not attacking. It knew that waiting for the rest of the pack would increase its odds. It snarled, lips peeling back to reveal canines dripping with saliva, yellow eyes flecked with gold stared back at him intelligently.

Trevor knew he could not afford to wait. Screaming at the top of his lungs he attacked. The wolf was caught off guard by Trevor's sudden assault. In its surprise it hesitated, and as it attempted to turn and retreat, the spear tip pierced its flank. It yelped as it was skewered in the ribs. Trevor drove forward pushing the spear deeper, past ribs to muscles and organs; the wolf contorted its body into a U shape, attempting to bite at the offending spear, and when it saw the impossibility of that, it changed tactics, attempting with a lunge to attack its attacker. Both attempts were futile, and Trevor continued to push the damaged wolf to the edge of the stream. Something flashed in its eyes, something Trevor did not like, its body seemed to expand, lengthening, thickening, but he kept driving forward, not sure of what he was seeing. He drove the beast into a pool of deeper water, pushing it under the dark red surface, trying to hold it down as it thrashed in an attempt to get its snout above water to snatch vital air.

The water frothed as the thrashing continued, going from translucent red to opaque crimson as blood mixed with the moss-tainted water. And in that swirling syrup of red he thought he saw a monster rising from the red pool, something large, with a long snout and large curved teeth and needle-like hair thick and rigid as a porcupine's quills. His mind began to regain focus, the blood pool centering him, his heart slowing, his breathing returning to normal.

The remaining beasts were circling behind him, he could hear them but now he had access to the darkta and knew that these were no normal animals of the forest. They were not really wolves or at least were not only wolves. There essence was something else. Removing the spear, he turned to stare at the four other monsters that were beginning to pace in a semicircle toward him. He stepped into the shallow water near the waterfall, putting his back close to the rocks, which offered him some protection. He had his spear clutched tightly in his right hand and his long curved dagger with its serrated edge in his left. These creatures' darkta energy patterns were the same. They were beasts but they had been modified by the ancients' sorcery to be something more. They were capable of taking on other shapes and had the intelligence of a murderous human but with the single-minded, starving animal instinct for hunting prey. He had no doubt the witch had sent them, imprinting his scent and appearance in their minds, driving them mad till they could think only of killing him. He could see the spark of her spell arching behind their eyes. Their hot breath plumed before them. The pair to his left began to transform, he could hear bones shifting, skin stretching. They raised their heads to the sky and let loose an otherworldly cry of pain as their bodies reformed.

Facing the other creatures, he watched in horror as their physiques were transmuted. One wolf stood upright on lengthened hind legs, looking like an ostrich but with a lean muscular torso; its head grew narrow, its jaw forming a sharp beak. Its previously soft hair grew thick and wiry, rows of black needles sticking straight up from its back. He knew that thick barbed hair would puncture skin and draw blood if he touched it. It moved its long neck back and forth, shoving its long deadly beak out in front of him like a bird of prey.

The animal to his far left had transformed into a beast with long rear legs that leaned forward, almost like a kangaroo he had seen in a picture book about the south lands. But this creature's legs were capable of holding its torso out almost parallel to the ground as it poked a reptile-shaped head toward him and opened up its maw to reveal several rows of teeth. His father had told him stories of dragons as a boy, and this is what his young mind had pictured when listening to those stories, although this monster lacked the wings those fabled creatures were said to have.

The two creatures in the center of his vision expanded, growing to double the size of a normal wolf with thick heavy muscles and elongated jaws. Trevor began to feel fear again and the darkta symbols became jumbled. He tried to concentrate and regain control of the darkta, needing to find the flow state Rakesh had told him was essential during combat. When the bird of prey sprang forward there was no more time, there was no thinking, preparing, there was only reaction.

Its webbed feet allowed it to move rapidly toward him over the water. In a moment it was within attacking distance, thrusting that dagger beak at him. Its long neck was capable of multiple levels of movement, up, down, right, left, swiveling freely on its axis at the base of the neck. The first attack he could do nothing but duck, the second he half parried with his spear while dodging to his right, which put him face to face with the razor-rimmed mouth of the dragon, its scaled skin glistening, its breath that of decaying meat as it roared at him and then bit down, the target his right arm. He pulled back and moved away but now every move right and left forced him into the sphere of attack of one of the other monsters. The large wolves were entering the stream, picking out the shallow areas as they made their way toward the battle. The river had slowed them down as he had hoped, the deeper pools forcing them to take a roundabout path through the shallows, but it would not stop them. He sliced at the dragon's neck, his blade barely cutting through the scales, but it was enough of an annoyance that the head rose up and turned to the left, which exposed its yellow reptilian eye. He sank the dagger home, pushing it deep into the eye socket. The creature reared up sharply. The combination of wet hands and shaky nerves made Trevor lose hold of the dagger. It was ripped from his hands, the pommel sticking out from the socket like a distended pupil. He grabbed at the backup on his hip as the wolves closed in. The bird pecked, and he was able to land a glancing blow to its flank with his fist buying him just enough time to throw the blade at the first wolf. He heard it yelp as the blade found its mark and then returned his attention to the attacking beak of the bird, but it was too late. The bird had lunged forward after backing up momentarily and sank its pointed beak into his left shoulder.

The pain was terrible, hitting nerves that sent shock waves of pain up his neck. Lightning bolts of agony shot through his brain, but as they did, they set afire those mystic areas that put him in touch with the darkta. He felt the warm radiation of energy between his eyes. The pain receded and suddenly he was able to dissect all the components, both physical and magical, used to create the monsters. As though sliding and manipulating the panels of a puzzle box, he reached out with his open hand clasping a component near the creature's long neck and slid a bolt out of place, unlocking the magical protection, which allowed his fingers to slide between and behind dimensions and manipulate the physical layer beneath. Squeezing hard Trevor broke its neck, collapsing its esophagus. As it tried to scream and draw breath through its shattered windpipe he annihilated the illukta energy that pumped at its core with a darkta spell. With the core destroyed, the rest of its being began to collapse and unfold. He pulled a curved knife from his leg sheath and brought his right arm across in a slicing arc. The curved blade cut through the creature's neck as though it were composed of nothing more than smoke. The real work had already been done; the killing stroke was more of a symbolic formality. The decapitated body fell into the deeper parts of the pool, which was now a swirling opaque dark red, its blood added to that of Trevor's first victim.

The dragon and one of the wolves were coordinating their attacks; he could see the magical symbols and runes pass between them, communicating their plan as they both lunged at him from different angles simultaneously. His pierced left arm dangled uselessly from its socket, and there was no way he could defend himself with only his right arm and the knife. But the pain and adrenaline had unlocked a new form of consciousness that now directed him. Not only did he have access to the darkta but there was a flow to his actions that did not require conscious direction, as though all things were happening as they were meant to happen and could not happen differently. Time dilated, slowing to a drip. He faced the rock shelf and loosened the tight chemical bonds that made it solid. Both the dragon's head and the wolf's hit the rock of the waterfall as he ducked below their floundering arms. The granite gave as though it were nothing more than mud. There was a sucking sound as their heads entered the mud. Trevor began to manipulate the chemical bonds again. The creatures' legs scrambled for purchase as they tried to pull themselves from the hardening muck. There was a sound of bones breaking; legs and torsos flailed in pain. The thrashing quickly turned to a quiver as he fit the quantum pieces back together, the mud becoming solid granite again. The bodies gave one final death tremor before going lifeless. Their rears and legs hung from the granite, backward trophies.

He turned to the last wolf, which was backing away, hunched low, looking afraid and contemplating flight. It stared at him not as prey now but as predator. Trevor was burning with energy, steam coming off his body, skin smoking in the turbulent air. Blood from his wounds dripped down his exposed torso, the head of the bird creature is still hanging from his shoulder the beak buried deep within the muscle, its opened neck dripping gore into the stream. Trevor had been transformed into a monster, the darkta energy pulsing through him making him something more. He pushed the knife back into its sheath and used his free hand to pull the beak from his shoulder with a low grunt, dropping the head at his feet, never taking his eyes off the remaining wolf.

He flipped the spear to his left hand, tested its weight with his odd hand, and smiled. Smiled because this had suddenly become a game he knew he would win, it was just a matter of how. The wolf turned to run and Trevor launched the spear while simultaneously manipulating the creature's makeup, taking away the magical defenses and loosening the physical bonds of its armor; the spear entered the bullseye of its anus like a bolt of lightning and exploded from its mouth, entrails, lungs, and trachea all obliterated as it passed through. The wolf fell silently and lifelessly to the ground. A sadistic smile was plastered on Trevor's face. It had a dark twist to it that mimicked the grin of the witch.

The witch had lied about the start and the rules of the game. This attack made it clear that from here on out there were no rules, no deals. He washed out his wounds in the water. Focused on the darkta energy he attempted to modify the molecules of his skin to close the larger wound in his shoulder but seemed unable to do anything but make very minor adjustments. He could see the spells but could not seem to place them in the right configuration, maybe there was too much adrenaline or anger causing his mind to quake and that was just enough to thwart his attempts. He took out the needle and thread that Rakesh had made him use to patch his training wounds and awkwardly stitched himself up.

The battle had been good. It had given him new confidence. After he had killed the first creature in a moment of panic he had been able to calm his mind enough to conjure his own darkness and utilize it to obliterate the light. It had been a test of both his warrior and mystical abilities and both had proven up to the challenge. The darkness and the monster hiding within had been revealed.

He slept. He did not dream. The witch did not visit him.

Chapter 10

The next morning, he packed up his gear and resumed his trek up the summit. The stream ended at the glacial ice. He filled his canteen once more in the rust-colored stream, suddenly contemplating whether just drinking from the water that ran through the red moss had placed enough of the psychoactive compound in his body to cause him to hallucinate. Had all this been a drug-induced stupor that had begun when he had ingested the mystical potion that had allowed him to see the darkta? It had all seemed so surreal and insane and yet he had taken it in stride, as though he had had his reality turned upside down every day of his life, conversing with animated flames, seeing cyclopean tree spirits, fighting monsters.

He gazed at his reflection in the pool of water and did not recognize himself. There was a stony hardness to his face, deep creases in his brow, slate-gray eyes hardened by sadness that had seen too much, so much they would never be able to unsee. He tried to picture himself as he once was, easy-going with a broad relaxed smile, quick to hug, give a pat on the back, laugh. He could not. Had that life been the dream? Was that part of him dying, eclipsed and choked by the rising darkness? In his eyes he searched deeper for his true loves and saw them slipping behind the gray shadows of his memory, Jake smiling at him as he tousled his hair playfully, Lydia staring up at him with those huge brown eyes that seemed to hold an entire universe in them. Then there was Mary, with that deep soulful glint in her eyes. In her eyes, he would see the man she loved, the man he had struggled to become.

He rummaged through his rucksack and removed the tin containing the ashes of his home. Opening the lid, he brought it to his nose and smelled fresh cornbread, Jake's hair, Lydia's baby skin, Mary's breath. The memories swarmed and coalesced around him and he knew that life had been no dream. He still carried them with him. Rakesh had tattooed his victims' essence into his skin and Trevor had tattooed them into his mind and soul. That was how he would carry them through this dark journey to wherever it took them. Heaven? Salvation? He did not know if heaven existed or if salvation was possible, but he would bring them to this journey's end and as a family they would confront the thing that had turned their dreams into a nightmare. Splashing water on his unfamiliar reflection he turned away from what lay in the past. There were no more answers to be found there. The only way out was through.

By afternoon he was approaching the summit. His feet were cold, the ice he trod upon invading his boots, worming its way into his feet and into his blood. He had not brought enough food and the thin air at this altitude made breathing difficult. He had drunk all his water; his mouth was constantly dry. He knew he needed to reach the summit quickly so he could descend before he succumbed to hypothermia.

When he reached the summit he gazed down upon a beautiful scene. A long valley stretched out before him, another glacial stream meandered down the mountain's face to a river that cut the valley in two, farther off were pine forests, and farther in the distance he saw a village, or at least the remains of one, moss-covered slate roofs poking through layers of fog. It was far away but he thought he could see smoke rising into the purple-orange-yellow light of the setting sun. So much color. So much life. For a moment the shadow the witch had cast receded, and the world was all brightness and light, filled with beauty, hope, and possibility. He forgot all the horror, all the things that had happened to bring him to this point and felt redeemed. He let the setting sun burn his eyes, its image traced into his retinas even as he closed them and passed out from hunger and exhaustion.

The first thing Trevor was aware of when he woke was that he could not see the stars or moon. He was inside or underneath something. Again there was that surreal quality to his senses; he could not determine whether he was awake or asleep. Time ticked, he was quiet, unmoving, trying to extend his senses and determine where he was. Gradually his senses awoke and he felt the heat of a fire to his left, smelled the smoke, heard the crackling of the wood as it expanded and charred. He was warm, comfortable, swaddled in blankets. After so many months of being cold, the warmth and feel of the blankets was blissful. His mouth and throat were dry but after so many months of pain and anguish, of being tested day and night, of being beaten, thrown naked into the cold, every inch of him in a constant state of hurt, this was heaven. He was warm and rested. He had no idea what had saved him or what its intentions were, but for a moment he was content with just the feeling of warmth. He breathed slowly, meditatively; he did not want to give away the fact that he was awake and did not want to move till he had some idea of where he was or who might be with him. If it is the Coma Witch or one of her minions he might be attacked once they knew he was conscious.

Ever so slowly he turned his head to the left in the direction of the fire and the breathing that he heard. He kept his eyes closed, feigning sleep, and reached for the knife that he hoped was still on his hip and realized he was naked.

"I already know that you are awake." A voice of distant rolling thunder that booms in his ears.

Trevor opened his eyes. The face he saw beyond the fire looked ancient. Deeply etched lines and scars cut across the leathery landscape of his face, a map of pain and sadness. But the almond-colored eyes, flecked with gold that shines in the light of the fire, held hope, joy. They seemed to pulse in the flickering light of the fire, surging out in waves that then crash against the deep grooves of his cheeks and forehead. Long gray hair hung down to the man's chest and framed his face. He expanded as he sat upright and Trevor could see that he was huge, a colossus in a world of mere men.

"I found you on the summit. No man can survive the night up there exposed to the wind and cold. Even in spring it will kill hearty men."

"Thank you"

"I gather you are after the witch?"

"I am."

The giant grunted and shifted his gaze back to the flames.

"Seems the only people that cross that mountain nowadays are either the witch herself, someone chasing her, or someone performing some errand on her behalf." The giant's gaze shifted from the fire out into the night landscape, searching, reminiscing. "Used to be that people would cross on a pilgrimage or quest of some spiritual import but those days are gone I guess."

Trevor waited as the giant paused, his eyes continuing to search the darkness outside.

"Whatever you've seen or done up till now is but a taste. What comes next will be hell. From here on out you will not know who to trust, what is a trap or a potential weapon. From here on the witch owns you and the world you travel through."

"Was that her message?"

"Probably. I didn't ask as she passed nor did she bother with me. I'm an observer nothing more. Most involved I get is saving someone from freezing to death and then talking their ear off." He smiled at his own self-effacing wit. Trevor grinned, finding the giant easy to trust even though he had just been told that no one could be trusted from this point on. The fact that he could have simply killed Trevor but did not was not lost to him. If the giant had wanted him dead he would already be dead.

"It's just how I've seen it. How I continue to see it. I'm not of her. Never have been. Hope never to be."

He turned his gaze back to Trevor who found himself fidgeting under the giant's scrutiny, the fiery gaze making him uncomfortable.

"I live up here. Great view. I can look east and see the past, look west and gaze into the future, and right here I get to live in my own eternal moment untouched by either." He paused to take a deep breath and then continued, "I see you coming from the east and I know you're living in the past, your life is under her spell, in a coma, suspended in limbo until you catch up to her. But until that time you're back there," he bent his elbow, his thumb pointing over his shoulder to the east. "And you're here now. Passed out from exhaustion in sight of such a prophetic view, staring out at your future as far as your eyes can see, the valley, the village of monsters and phantoms, the mountain range and whatever lies beyond. And then after all that, if you make it that far, there is HER. The horizon stretching out to eternity. But still you feel her pull. I see it in your eyes. The fever of desire to kill her to end her reign of terror over you. To kill the darkness that haunts you."

"If you can see it, then what is my future?" Trevor demanded.

"To chase. What results from that, pain, death, damnation, redemption will be determined by your choices during the chase. But there is only one path to her. Through the valley, through the village of monsters and phantoms which is almost certain death. It is filled with comas like yourself, lost to the darkness. As she passed through I have no doubt she repoisoned their minds to torture you in some fashion. Make you turn back or kill you if they can't convince you to do so. And if that fails or she feels you are a worthy adversary she may even unleash the monsters and phantoms. The comas are nothing compared to them. Some of the choices in this game are hers as well."

"I won't be turned back."

"Nope. I can see that."

"Then what choice do I have?"

"She's showing you the darkness. She opened the doors of hate and despair. Then your desire for revenge grew and you found sorcery to manipulate it. I know Rakesh and what he does. I had a similar conversation with him way back in the day."

"Is that why he went back?"

"Never crossed the summit. He turned back before gazing at the future. But yeah, maybe. Maybe he could see it before he saw it, saw the darkness stretching out before him and knew what it would do."

"So its giving up or going on?"

"Or redemption. There is miracle to your sorcery. You've channeled the darkta but there is also the illumika, born of the positive energies that combine and heal. The illukta and darkta are in conflict and the combination is one of annihilation. But the illumika is a higher-order energy that transforms and heals. It sees all energy as energy, not as dark and light."

The giant paused again, while staring at him, searching for understanding in Trevor's eyes. "May I show you?"

Trevor was uncertain, but nodded.

"Sit up and get closer to the fire."

Trevor did so. The tent they were in was warm; there was a hole overhead for the smoke and the front flap yawned open to the valley, the darkness of the forest below, and the twinkling of stars above. He could tell by his breathing and the amount of oxygen he was able to take in with each breath that they must be thousands of feet below the summit.

The ceiling of the tent was braced by pine branches, and boughs covered with animal skins formed the ceiling. The skins had been rubbed smooth and tanned; they gleamed like marble in the glow of the fire. Trevor sat with his legs crossed and stared at his host, waiting.

"Let me show you."

A huge fist reached out from the flames emerging from the heart of the flickering fire, large fingers unfurling, index finger flying toward him as it uncurled. Cross-eyed, Trevor followed the finger's trajectory as it landed with infinite gentleness and impossible kindness between his eyes.

And the world changed.

White light replaced everything. There was nothing else. The light was warm, embracing, all encompassing. There was no need in it, no want; it was perfect in its completeness, lacking nothing. There was no him there was only All, and this frightened him. The light wavered and there was color and shadow to it. "I!" he screamed into the light for fear that he would be swallowed if he did not make his presence known to both the light and himself. It flooded into him and was warm, comforting. He sighed, he breathed, and the world colored with golden light came into focus, sparks of energy leaping from one surface to another.

His benefactor looked at him from across the flames, eyes sparkling like diamonds, "The light is the truth. We create the shadows. We project the world through our fears and experience the darkness created by our delusional egos."

Trevor gazed wide-eyed across the hut, out through the opening into the darkness beyond, and then up at the twinkling stars; there were networks of strings connecting each to the other, creating a heavenly net that connected with the mountain, the trees, the ground, him—divine, golden energy flooding behind even those things that had seemed dark.

"The darkness is easy to find. Humanity is hardwired to see it. Our fear, our anger, our violence expands it. But we are more than just human. Deep down we carry with us the spark of deity and as deity we must create and what we create we project. The manipulation of darkness is sorcery, creating and recreating, The Lie. There is no sorcery in light, only truth."

The giant now looked more closely at Trevor's right eye, examining it with a fixed gaze. Trevor felt pressure, that same feeling of his eye protruding outward, being pulled or torn from his socket. "What are you staring at?" Trevor asked him, growing uneasy and self-conscious under this surgical stare. The giant touched his forehead again and the light disappeared.

"She is pulling you into the darkness, feeding your hate. The illukta and darkta are not a choice, they are of the same system. The true choice is between the delusional system of illukta and darkta or that of illumika. One system cannot exist in the presence of the other. You see either one or the other. Illumika is of love and only loves perfectly, it can only forgive and heal, it cannot serve dark needs or exist in shadow. This is the choice."

He paused for a moment, then filled the void with his thundering voice, "Rest."

His words carried physical weight and Trevor found his lids closing, his breathing deepening, and he fell uncontrollably into sleep within moments.

Chapter 11

Trevor opens his eyes and Mary is lying before him naked upon a mound of soft, lush moss. Around her flowers of various hues scream violent, beautiful colors. She is calling him forward. Light dances across the pollen that fills the air, her white skin shimmers like marble in the sun. She smiles. He so loved her smile, how it had the ability to save any day, to turn turmoil into joy. It had been her gift.

She sits up as he approaches and he begins to run toward her, his fingers already feeling the phantom touch of her skin, the smell of her. From behind Mary, rising from the bed of moss is the witch, her presence a scar upon the perfection of this beauty. Light is flickering playfully across Mary's skin, glowing, a golden nimbus surrounding her. She does not react as the witch runs the long curved jagged nail of an index finger across her alabaster throat. Blood so dark it looks black streams down her throat, running down between her breasts, a dark river bisecting her torso.

Trevor screams soundlessly, Mary's head tilts backward, light pouring from the gaping wound. The witch puts her chin on Mary's shoulder, half of her face hidden behind the dark crown of Mary's hair. Her left eye is gaping, turning aqueous as the light from Mary's neck is sucked into the swirling vortex, flashing white-hot as Mary's essence is annihilated in the dark matter of the witch's eye. There is a final flash and Mary's body is falling backward, lifeless. The witch smiles at him crookedly and with her murderous index finger taps at the obsidian eye transmuted from liquid to glass, the nail clinking on its surface, reflecting his fear and anguish back at him. She winks, upper lid falling like a guillotine blade across the expanse of her eye. The world disappears. Trevor blinks and opens his eyes.

The giant hermit was standing on a rock outcropping overlooking the long valley that stretched to the distant mountains. This was the first time Trevor witnessed him standing at his full height. He is huge, at least eight feet tall. His body is thick and heavily muscled. Trevor had heard rumors of beings that had been created by the ancients using special magic. They had tried to create physically superior beings to serve as workers, warriors, and assassins by manipulating their bodies with special potions and rituals. In the legends these creatures were extremely strong and difficult to wound or kill. They became the focus of many grandiose stories, small groups of colossi killing entire armies or laying waste to entire cities. It was another example of the ancestors' techknowledgy growing out of their control. The colossi became part of the legend of the End, when the world turned backward, the techknowledgy stopped working, and those who were left turned away from their ancestors' sorcery. It was then that techknowledgy became associated with evil. The old ways were to be feared and avoided. But some of the dark creatures created by that sorcery remained, the colossus was one, and now Trevor began to theorize that the witch was another—born from the fires of that ancient alchemy, "techknowledgy."

Trevor wondered if the giant was a descendant of the colossi or if he had been built so perfectly that he had survived the centuries and would continue centuries longer till his body finally began to give way to nature. He did not ask. But he wondered how lonely that would be, to go on and on with no one to share your life with, to hope each day that time would simply end so you could be released. The colossus spoke, ending his contemplation.

"You have made your decision."

It was not a question.

The giant raised his arms to point at the village, which looked to be many miles away. "The village is black poison, death. And you must cross it. Follow the scar of the valley, where glaciers once cut through. These lowlands will be swampy and treacherous but keeping to them will prevent you from getting lost, which is easy to do in the pine forests where everything begins to look the same covered and cloaked in mist. You can spend a week walking in a circle. Beyond the village will be the mountains and beyond them the end of the world as we know it. That is her world."

He said no more, simply stood stoically, unmoving, surveying the valley.

Trevor gathered his things and walked down the mountain into the swamp.

The lowlands from one end of the valley to the other were cloaked in a perpetual low-hanging thick fog. From atop Blood Mountain, as one looked out over the valley with the sun beginning to rise in the east, the mist looked like a gray soupy lake that covered the valley floor, and by midmorning the fog would settle into the trees. But it never went away. In the afternoon it covered the ground in thin vaporous tatters that obscured the ground. It made for slow progress.

The swamp would have been difficult enough without the visibility issues the fog created. One step fell in shallow water where a tangled web of roots passed for sure footing, the next step his foot disappeared into a deep hole, soaking him up to his thigh, mud sucking at his foot, ensnaring him as his other foot twisted trying to maintain a precarious balance on roots covered in moss and swamp slime. In some cases he could right himself, and in others he fell face forward, his hands searching for purchase, his spear hilt searching for solid ground to act as a balancing point. Eventually he would push himself upright and take another awkward step. He cursed, his breathing ragged, the effort and frustration sapping both his physical and mental energy.

By late afternoon he was almost through what he hoped would be the worst of it. The promise of solid ground appeared in the distance as taller pine trees with green healthy needles replaced the rotted and stunted trees of the swamp. The sun had already begun to set, the mist thickening. The sight of the pines enlivened him. He quickened his pace, his mind imagining the feel of drier ground. It was then that the figure appeared, arising from the mist as Trevor was struggling forward. It was a man standing in hip-deep water. He had long tangled hair and a thick beard and his uncovered torso was wiry and firm. The ax in his hands and the fist clenched around the handle ready to unleash a killing stroke made his intentions clear. Trevor stopped in his tracks and stared at the man, whose brown eyes looked sad instead of fierce.

They stood that way in silence. A standoff in the receding light, neither man seeming to want to make the first move. Trevor unclipped the snap on his dagger's scabbard. The sound boomed in the silence and the man flinched, his muscles contracting as he raised the ax to his shoulder. His mouth slackened and his eyes glared, not with violence or anticipation but with fear. This was not one of the Coma Witch's minions; it was a cursed man trying to live up to whatever promise he had made. Trevor instantly felt sorry for him and eased the grip on his spear. This did not have to end in death.

"We don't have to do this. Whatever she promised you is a lie. Just turn around," Trevor said softly.

"Did you? Would you?"

"I didn't. That is how I know she and everything about her is a lie."

"And yet here we are."

Trevor had no response to that. With all that he knew, he was still choosing to chase the witch.

"She has the souls of my family and won't release them. She killed them on my first refusal and now is threatening them with torture beyond the grave if I don't fulfill my promise."

"Just turn around. Nothing she says is true. She only follows through on her curses, not her promises."

"She'll know if I don't try to kill you. I'm sure she is watching even now." He paused, swallowing, "I must do what she asks. She told me to tell you that I am innocent, a pawn, and to go on you must kill me."

"And what if I don't. What if I just incapacitate you and move on."

"I will pursue you until I am dead for the sake of my family. If you tie up my arms, I'll cut them off to pursue you. She will free me, heal me, do whatever is needed until you kill me or I kill you." He paused, letting the implication sink in. "I ask you not to put me through that. I am your gateway to her. Either you or I must die."

Trevor grimaced. This was her game and she owned all the pieces and the board they played on.

The cursed man raised his ax and with a loud cry ran through the deep water toward Trevor. His movements were clumsy, and when he swung his ax from too far out it was easy for Trevor to sidestep. The man was muscled from farm work or some other occupation; he was not a warrior or soldier. With his second attempt he swung the ax downward. Trevor stepped to the side, easily avoiding it. He knew this could not go on and he knew what he had to do. The man was right, to prolong this was just delaying the inevitable. Neither he nor the man would turn from his purpose.

Trevor removed the dagger from its scabbard and plunged the tip into the man's chest, piercing his heart. The man looked into his eyes, his mouth hung open as he gasped for breath.

Trevor pulled the dagger from his chest, feeling hot blood run over his hands. "I'm sorry," Trevor whispered. "Be free now."

The man's eyes closed and Trevor let the body slip below the surface of the water, the swamp claiming him. His fingers were covered with blood, innocent blood. He told himself that killing him had been a mercy but he also knew that he had crossed yet another line. If he had turned back, if he had given up his vengeance, this man could have lived. But to complete this quest he would have to kill all in his path. He was no longer what he once was and realized that his quest had morphed into something more than a vendetta. He wanted answers, he wanted to know what the witch was and her motives for doing what she did. His quest had evolved to include metaphysical curiosity. If he understood her, her shadow, maybe this would all make sense, and armed with this knowledge he would find a chance for redemption. Redemption for him, his family, this man, maybe the world. His father had always said that knowledge was power and he wanted to know if that was true. If knowing a thing gave you power over it and allowed you to transcend it.

He pushed the questions aside, allowing them to sink into the noxious water the same way the dead body had, and moved forward through the final fifty yards of swampy muck, finally reaching ground that, while not dry, at least was not covered in thigh-high water and thick mud.

The air was damp, chilling him, and he quickly gathered fallen branches for a fire. He started with the branches that had been dangling from lower limbs instead of those lying in the damp earth to use as kindling. But even these were difficult to get going. The moisture of fog and earth made its way into the very core of everything. Flint and steel would not work, and after a period of mounting frustration, he finally resorted to using the gas torch Rakesh had gifted him to get the kindling started. Once the kindling was smoking and crackling with heat, he moved the torch away and then shook it before placing it back in the rucksack. It contained enough for maybe one more fire, two at most, and then it would be gone, and he doubted he would find another artifact like it on the last leg of this journey. He shrugged, what option did he have? When it was gone it was gone. At least he had had it to get this fire started; he needed the warmth of a fire tonight, the cold and wet was seeping into his bones. The fire would only smolder the flames grudgingly, lapping at the damp wood. He had to almost shove his hands into the flames to feel the heat, but again, it was something. If nothing else, it stopped the progress of the cold.

He sat and watched the lengthening shadows as the sun set. Before the thick mist rose into the lower branches of the pines he caught glimpses of a swirling cluster of stars. He tried to conjure the golden light of the illumika. The illuminated net was pulled over the world momentarily and then quickly disappeared. He tried to manifest it again and struggled to manipulate the strands of energy but managed only to connect a few stars. The damp cut into his concentration, making him shiver, eating away at his psyche. There was no use in fighting it now; he needed to conserve his energy for defense and attack. He gave up with a frustrated sigh, but the momentary vision gave him hope, because he realized that the healing light of the illumika was ever present even when he could not see it.

The mist rose, the moonlight slithering over its surface, the air swirling with blue-white light. The smoky mist pulled back, revealing darkness, and then swirled in again in thick clouds, as though the forest was a pair of giant lungs breathing in and out. It mesmerized him, allowing him to forget the cold. He rested his back against the trunk of one of the pines, the embers winking at him as he struggled to relax, closing his eyes in search of peace.

The giggling is so distant that at first he thought he was imagining it. As it grew closer he knew its source. Mary and Jake, playing a game of hide-and-seek from the beyond. A few yards away Jake pokes his smiling face from around a tree, giggling. "You're it Dad," and then he disappears. Trevor can hear his running feet moving away and then circling.

"Peek-a-boo!" from his left. His wife naked, seductively appearing from behind a tree, leaning forward, breasts swinging. She puts an arm out in front of her that seems to grow and stretch toward him, palms up, index finger curling in a come-hither gesture. Lips pursed, eyes lit with passion. She giggles and runs away, her hips swaying, her ass glowing in the light of the moon, receding. Trevor does not move. Tears well up in his eyes, and he reminds himself of the promise he had not lived up to of not shedding another tear, but the despair runs so deep, cutting him in half, tearing his soul apart.

"Daddy! You're it!"

"Please, Trevor, chase me."

He is crying. Mary runs across an open expanse, hiding behind the next tree, where she disappears. There is a silent moment laced with misery and then he watches in horror as the witch runs silently across the same expanse, giving chase where he refused. This absolutely silent pursuit is somehow so much more unsettling than her usual loud cackling. There is no sound in her swift movement, as though she were hovering over the ground in pursuit.

His son appears around a distant tree and the witch rises from behind him, enfolding him, swallowing him into her darkness, the black eye staring at Trevor. His own eye twitches, swelling, the pressure mounting. His son is gone and the witch folds and crumples into the blackness—gone.

His wife circles around a tree and then rushes toward him, her hands outstretched, as though she is asking Trevor to save her. When she gets within a few feet of him she is suddenly pulled backward, her hands and feet thrown toward him as she is bent at the waist, her body stretching into a U. "Trevor," she whispers and is then pulled backward, ass first, the witch swallowing her in her shadow. Mary is gone.

The witch's eye swirls with clouds of darkness that form a cyclone that tears apart her own body, like a serpent eating its own tail, till she is nothing more than a black swarm of particles that buzz like flies as they circle the eye. The eye pulls this swarm into itself, swells, and then explodes silently into nothingness—gone.

Trevor closes his tear-filled eyes not wanting to see anymore.

When he opened his eyes in the morning the mist was swirling around his legs, thick with particles of frost. He did not want to think about the previous night. He just wanted to move on, to complete his quest as quickly as possible. He picked up his rucksack and started walking.

The forest is much easier to trek than the swamp and he made good time. By the evening he made it to the top of a small hillock that overlooks the village the colossus had warned him about.

"Death and insanity," the giant hermit had told him. But there was nothing ominous for him to see. The mist covered the streets. The buildings or portions of them that he could make out were indistinct but looked dilapidated. Moss covered the gray and black stones of walls and slate roofs. In many places pieces of wall or roof were missing. In some cases, the moss was so thick there were mushrooms and swamp flowers growing upon the slanted roofs or the hollowed-out sections of wall.

Poking through the lake of mist was the long metal rod of one of the ghost-talk towers. It was leaning precariously as if pointing at him. He could only see the top of it, but its presence made him feel uneasy, as he was reminded of all the stories his grandfather had told him about the strange towers. Grandfather's stories contained more myth than those of

Trevor's pragmatic, logical father who would try to relay the scientific understanding of the ancients' objects. "They broadcast demons and ghosts through the air that would carry messages. Ghosts whispering in your ear, flying around you all the time. And they made these special devices that could capture their voices and fill your head with them." Trevor shuddered, wondering not for the first time what the ancients had been thinking when creating such things. The presence of these towers was always a bad omen, as though their malicious intent continued to haunt the air surrounding them. It was not good finding one outside a dark village that he was told would bring only death and insanity.

He heard nothing. It was a ghost town, but he felt its darkness. There was a weight to the air, a coldness that told him the hermit was correct, this was a place of insanity and death, but he had also been correct in saying Trevor had to pass through. He was being drawn here. He sat. He would wait till morning. He laid back, not bothering with a fire. Exhaustion claimed him. The witch visited him in his dreams but only to taunt him with that perverse sadistic grin and ear-splitting cackle. There was no need for more, he was in her web now.

In the morning his wife leaned over to plant a delicate kiss on his lids, waking him. As he emerged from the haze of sleep she became smoke dispersing into the early morning light. The mist screened the sky from view, the sun sent columns of light to pierce the gray blanket. He scanned the scene around him seeing even less of the village than he had seen the night before. Only the twisted metal of the ghost-talk tower was visible, the spear upon its top poking through the thick haze. If he was going to see anything else or learn anything else, he would have to enter the village. Remote observation was not going to yield any epiphanies.

He picked up his gear, making sure he was armed with his spear and that his knives were in easy reach, and then headed down the small hill and entered the village of phantoms and monsters.

The main street was cobbled stone slick with moss. The mist was so thick he could only see twenty or thirty feet in front of him, the stone structures rising slowly from the mist. The rounded stones of the buildings were piled atop one another, held together by grout or cement. One of the buildings was constructed of large stones that were cut perfectly at right angles, with perfect edges and intricate symbols carved into their surfaces. This was obviously the work of the ancients. The tools needed to perform such work were either no longer in existence or had run down with no one alive with the knowledge or inclination to fix them. Some of the symbols he had seen in the darkta. Examining the symbols, he began to wonder if the ancients had more knowledge of the darkta than he did and if what Rakesh had passed on to him was limited in comparison or had it grown and developed since the ancients had tapped into its power? Had the ancients created this town? Which made him wonder if they were responsible for whatever darkness inhabited this place. Were they the ghosts poisoning the air, broadcast from the tower and now roaming the darkta unseen, waiting for an unwary traveler to come through? Were he and the witch nothing more than pawns in the ancients' perverted game of chess, the town, the tower, all of it just obstacles meant to torment them?

The sound of water dripping pulled his attention back to the now. Once he was attuned to it he heard it constantly, everywhere. Every surface was damp or covered in moss that oozed, water droplets pinging against stone or into small puddles, echoing, forming an ode to moisture that became a cacophony around him and put his nerves on edge. He knew that with constant exposure it could drive a man insane.

As he passed by one of the buildings he looked at its door, bare wood, nails popping out of its surface, the wood flaked and rotten. He detected motion out of the corner of his eyes and glanced toward the small window to the left of the door, swearing he saw a shadowy form, a face, peering out at him. Another motion directed his gaze to the second story and he could swear he had seen another face, white skin, black eyes, ethereal as smoke and then gone.

The sun had reached its zenith, burning away layers of mist that allowed him to see more of the broad main street he had been walking down. There was a row of five or so structures on each side of the cobbled street. At its terminus stood a church, evidenced by its architecture and the round stained glass window that hung above the large black double doors, a red pentagram hovering within a multicolored mosaic of blue, green, and yellow glass shards. The walls and edifices were constructed of gray stone. A large steeple rose at the rear of the church, where a large bell hung motionless. Rising behind the steeple stood the ghost-talk tower, its twisted dark structure looming over the church.

The mist suddenly turned thick and cold, coating his skin, forming small particles of frost on the hairs of his arm. He sensed something awful in the air, could taste it. It left a strange metallic taste on his tongue, a mixture of rust and blood. Then he heard music, a haunting melody in a minor key that deteriorated toward the atonal. One instrument sounded like an oboe, low and soft, and then a clarinet, a flute; syncopation, counter point, parallel arpeggios, weaving in and out in volume and tone, a dirge that plunged him into desolation, fear, and despair. He began to sweat in the frigid air, shaking. His head turned, searching for the music's origin. His soul had already determined what his ears were loath to confirm; the music was coming from the church.

Entranced, he continued to approach the gray structure, walking down the center of the main street. As he came to the next corner he glanced down the narrow alleyway. He heard a sound other than the music. A large stone was rolling across the alley, he followed its reverse path to a place where the mortar of the wall had cracked and given way. The stone continued to roll back and forth but he sensed there was something else there. It was not only the stone that had drawn his attention there was something else lurking in the shadows.

The stone came to rest on its base, silence settling in the alley. Nothing moved, but then he heard a sound like flesh slapping wetly against stone. That sick sound made the blood rage in his ears, his senses exploding as the sound seemed to thunder around him, approaching.

Pushing through the thick mist was an old man, ancient, wearing only a loincloth; black eyes peered from within deep, hungry sockets and his ashen skin was a thin sheet of onion paper stretched over brittle bones. Trevor could count each of the man's twenty-four ribs as they rattled in his torso, threatening to break apart as his feet slapped against the stone. He limped toward Trevor, one hand stretched out to Trevor beseechingly. Trevor could not move. Was this a ghost stitched together by the signals coming from the ghost towers, the ring of rectangular coffins at its apex opening and releasing souls to the trigger of the music? The man's white beard hid its mouth but he could hear him moan with each step, slap—*Ooooohhhh!* Trevor hefted his spear in front of him. He did not fear attack, he just did not want this decrepit ghost to touch him, fearing that it would somehow infect him with some type of sickness.

"Stop," Trevor commanded.

Amazingly, the man did.

"Please kill me," he pleaded in a raspy voice.

"What?" Trevor was dumbstruck.

"I've had enough. You're here because of her and the bell will toll and I don't want to be here for that again."

"Who is playing the music?"

He did not answer, "Pleassssse."

"Is that what you're afraid of, the music?" Trevor turned to look at the church and the old man took advantage of this distraction and threw himself upon the tip of Trevor's spear. His eyes gazed upward toward the sky and there was something of a smile on his face.

"Thank you," he gasped and fell to the ground.

Just as his body hit the cobbled street with a wet sickly slap the bell tolled. It was an awful sound, crashing through the air like the screech of a demon. It made Trevor grind his teeth as they vibrated in his mouth. His head ached, his ears protested, his stomach flipped, and he felt nauseous; bile rose in his throat. He felt faint and put the end of his spear on the ground to steady himself.

He turned his eyes to the bell tower. The vibrations from this awful device were visible; as they spread out they warped reality like a ripple across the surface of a lake. But the crests of these ripples contained a view into other dimensions.

"What is this?" Trevor asked of the mist.

The waves and troughs lengthened and he could see dark worlds unfolding in its undulations. Dark creatures roared, bloodthirsty and soul hungry. Some had black leathery skin, others sported hair or scales. There were creatures that looked like spiders with long legs and wolf heads and birds stripped of their feathers with pallid white skin and a reek of smoke, sulfur, and poison. The ground was black, the structures around him transformed into piles of rotting corpses. Piles of bones littered the street. Black diseased trees with long razor-sharp thorns covering their trunks and branches lined the street, flesh hanging from some of these spikes, heads skewered or hanging from the lower branches. He could smell the rot and gagged.

The wave crashed over him and he felt stripped raw as though the wave were abrasive sand peeling away his flesh, licking exposed neurons. The pain flared white-hot through his mind, his limbs lengthened, twisted, grew, turned black and powerful. And then it was gone for a moment as he entered a trough, but the next wave came, repeating the sequence but with less intensity, the waves strobing over the dark shores of his flesh and mind with decreasing force.

The bell tolled again, its chime painful to his ears. He glanced back at the church, the most intense wave washing over its surface transforming its gray moss and mold-covered stone into carved obsidian with sharp serrated surfaces and edges, intricate symbols etched over every inch came to light, burning low amber as the wave washed over the building, pulsing and strobing in the darkness. As the sound reverberated new instruments joined the haunting melody. A stringed instrument cried out from within the transformed church to join the deep moan of the oboe and clarinet, the flute paralleled its flight up a minor scale from low to high and then another gong as the bell tolled again, the more intense waves were now cresting and swallowing the weaker ones from the previous sounding of the bell. The distance between wave and trough shortened. The next wave hit him and it tore him apart, his body expanding, muscles and bones lengthening, thickening. Looking down at himself he saw a broadening chest, his skin turned a dark gray color, his clothes tore, unable to accommodate his increased bulk, and fell away in tatters.

Gong … the next wave. Gong … "Five," he began to count. Gong … "Six."

His mystic eye opened. Through darkta eyes he saw that his spear had been transformed; bringing it before his face for closer inspection, he could feel its power, could feel it pull at his bulging left eye. It was no longer a simple spear, it was a void in the dimensions, a vacuum that sucked in the energy surrounding it.

Gong ... "Seven."

The black doors of the dark temple were flung open and the creature playing the stringed instrument emerged, slithering out on a thick black tail. It had the torso of a naked female, full breasts, smooth dark green skin, exquisitely formed. It had a face that was threateningly beautiful, yellow catlike eyes stared out at him from beneath slithering hair that squirmed around her features like distressed snakes, standing straight up on her head for a moment and then continuing to caress her face. Forgetting the situation for a moment he became aroused by her presence. The creature had a dark allure. A visceral siren's call emanating from her, calling to something primal that stirred deep within him, a part of him that had been buried and denied for too long.

The rest of the demonic rabble fanned out to left and right of her as the music continued.

Gong ... "Eight." Gong ... "Nine."

The street was gone, the stone, the earth; it had all been transmuted by the toll of the bell or, maybe more precisely, exposed by it. The buildings were all carved from dark onyx with the magical symbols of the darkta covering every inch. Menacing trees with claws and roots that poked from the ground like tentacles flopped across the ground looking for fresh blood to spill. The heaps of rotting corpses, the piles of bones, the smell of rot, sulfur smoke, this place was death, it was insanity, it was hell.

The oboe player was a wolf/man dancing on huge legs with the torso of a thickly muscled man covered in black hair and the head of a wolf. The oboe pipe was stuck deep in its maw as it swayed and played. The clarinet player was the skeleton of a colossus, yellow bones creaking as it swayed back and forth, exposing the black swirling clouds of insects that served as its internal anatomy. The flute player was a naked woman, alabaster skin gleaming in the darkness and all the more enthralling and terrifying for it. Their instruments were alive, creatures that they seemed to be trying more to tame than play.

Gong … "Ten." The music reached a crescendo, the frenzy of the dance coming to a climax. They all seemed to be in the throes of some ecstasy, barely registering his presence.

Gong … "Eleven."

Gong … "Twelve."

Silence.

The reverberation washed over him. His body was covered in thick scales, he stood two feet taller, broad, his chin had lengthened, his nose and mouth pushed forward, his three eyes saw more of the world. Two eyes on the side of his head focused on the periphery and his mystic eye focused on what was before him and beyond and between; a 180-degree field of vision in which to sense attack. He breathed in deeply and felt powerful. Felt the dark energy from this body, from his dark weapons. The blackness from the earth seemed pulled up from the ground through his feet into his body, his left eye expanding again, but this time without pain. He felt … one with it … His weapons were an extension of him, he an extension of the dark energy surrounding him, a tuning fork vibrating in perfect synchrony with the darkta. His mystic eye saw the empty spaces between the illusion of the solid. This was the real him. The monster that had always been there, the mask that he had worn all his life had been ripped off by the toll of the bell, revealing the truth.

The four monstrous minstrels formed a line in front of the dark temple, the pentagram above them glowing red. Their instruments had completed their transformation into weapons. The wolf had a blade that was three feet wide and was almost as long as the wolf was tall; it looked impossible to lift. It held the handle in its extended right hand, its cleaver-shaped blade dragging along the ground behind him, scraping rocks and roots with a sound that made him shiver.

The alabaster-skinned witch swung a chain around her head like a lasso; at the free end three chains swirled outward with barbs along their length ending in five-inch pincers that glowed with a blue white light. He could hear the whistle of the weapon as it was swung expertly through the air at great speed in a blurring motion, and then at a flick of her wrist, the chain would straighten, the pincers flying out like arrows to strike their target. During the display she had plucked two eyes from one of the decapitated heads hanging from the tree. She would flick her wrist again, the chains snapping back with a cracking sound like a whip and then made to circle again, the cyclone of death whirling faster and faster with each turn.

The skeleton had a scythe with a red blade that glowed like molten lava, he swung the blade downward cleaving a rock in two, the halves rolling to the side the interior surface of each scorched and glowing an angry orange-red.

And the green goddess, the gorgon with hair wriggling frantically, wielded a long recurve bow made from the bone of a large monster. Its string was hewn from thick sinew still wet with blood and gore.

Four pairs of yellow eyes with black diamond-shaped pupils stared out at him, marking him. Yet he felt no fear. The transformation had been more than physical and he stared back into those hell born eyes ready for a fight.

The green-skinned gorgon moved with lightning grace, a bone arrow was nocked and flying toward him before he had registered that she had moved. If his senses had not been heightened and increased by his transformation, he doubted he would have seen anything. Without the time dilation that he experienced in the darkta, the best he could have hoped for would have been to see the arrow a split second before it bore into his skull, leaving him to wonder for that second how it had happened. But now every motion, every sound was important, it was extreme, his senses were heightened to such a fine point that that the arrow scarred the air, its point crackling through the air with energy as it annihilated and separated matter with its razor edges. Even so, the only reaction he had time for was to lean to his left, but it was not enough, the point missed its mark but the screeching blade ran along his cheek and tore off part of his earlobe as it flew past, warm blood ran down his neck.

In the one instant his eyes had been averted to escape the arrow, the quartet had fanned out to attack him from multiple angles, the gorgon nocking another arrow, the alabaster demon running to his left, her chains swirling overhead in a tornado spiral. Running toward him was the skeleton, fiery scythe raised. Trevor quickly scanned to his right for the werewolf but saw nothing of him and knew with hair-raising anticipation that it was circling behind him.

The gorgon had let loose her arrow as she screamed. Trevor dove to his right and rolled, avoiding both the arrow and the frontal assault of the skeletal wraith. Its bones creaked as it swung its molten scythe with a sound like the creak of ancient trees swaying in the wind. Trevor could hear the air sizzling as he narrowly ducked below the diagonal trajectory of the blade, which came within inches of his head. He could feel its blistering heat and smelled singed hair. Steam gushed from the damp black earth as the blade sunk deep into the ground, searing and cutting anything in its path.

Another arrow was flying toward him. He could sense it without directly seeing it, the molecules in the air prophesizing its path, which would end directly behind his right ear if he did not react. He could feel a slight pressure there, as though it had already happened, itching, scratching, telling him to move before it became a reality. He pulled his dagger from it place on his hip. He brought it up before him as he turned, the blade made of that same dark magic that had transformed his spear, a dimensional vacuum that hummed with dark purpose. He met the arrow's tip with the flat of the blade pulling it into the darkta; he continued his spin till he was again facing the wraith, who had managed to wrestle the molten scythe blade from the ground and was raising it behind him, preparing to swing, preparing to reap. Trevor flicked the edge of his blade over, the opposite flat end now facing his attacker. He pulled at the darkta directing it with his mind. The arrow, momentarily trapped between dimensions, held in stasis within the magical moment of the darkta created by the dagger, was unleashed. The arrow flew from the blade, as if entering one opened door and then released through another. It hit the wraith in the chest, finding its way between the gaps in its ribs. The creature staggered but nothing more; it swung the hooked red blade across its body, torso twisting, bones creaking and cracking loudly.

Trevor lunged back but the blade cut across his thigh burning. It was a deep cut and he shouted out. White-hot pain sprang from the wound and shot into his eyes, blinding him for a moment. He could hear the gorgon slithering toward him. The wraith's bones creaked anciently as it lunged toward him. The chains of the porcelain-skinned beauty reverberated through the air like a sonic boom with each pass growing closer. And then behind him he heard the heavy cleaver blade being dragged across stone by the werewolf. They were all converging on him.

The darkness enveloped him, feeding him. He took it in, his entire body and consciousness fueled by it. He turned to face the werewolf, the cleaver looming in the dark sky above. Trevor lunged toward it, his spear pushing forward, splitting the world as he thrust toward the wolf's throat. The heavy cleaver was a burden even for the enormous strength of this monster and the blade hung motionless at the blessed moment of its zenith, caught between rising and falling. The spear, knit from the threads of darkta, entered its throat and then went up under its jaw pushing farther into its head. The weapon swallowed matter, the blade humming and crackling with power, something within the creature popped, and then suddenly its body was crumpling up, folding in on itself like a piece of crumpled paper being crushed by an enormous fist until there was nothing left.

The gorgon's arrow entered his left shoulder, the point pushing out through the front but it hit nothing but flesh, a bad shot. He turned, the white witch's talon-tipped chains appearing from the storm of her controlled tempest like the claws of a monster. One pincer pierced his right bicep and another his ribs. One of the hooked barbs caught on the back side of his ribs, the bone cracking when she yanked it back. The serrated hook took bone and flesh with it, creating a hole in his side that bled profusely.

The wraith was swinging, all he could do was bend his torso backward at the waist, the blade cutting across his abdomen at the bottom of his ribs where the hole was, flesh burned and sizzled, blood steamed. He stood up straight. The wraith had put all its strength into the stroke hoping to cut him in half with its bones cracking as the blade continued its circular path, the wraith's body caught in the throws of its centrifugal force. As its body pivoted so that its side was vulnerable to him, Trevor lunged, raising his curved short sword to bring it down on the wraith's shoulder, separating its arm from its torso, the other arm continued in the swing, its waist twisting, looking as though it would spin from its pelvis under the strain and gravity of the blade. Trevor brought the blade down again, this time on the other shoulder, the blade flew outward taking the skeletal arm with it, bony fingers still clutching at the scythe's handle as the blade spun outward. Trevor ducked as it spun like a flying star over his head, and he knew without looking that the gorgon would be forced to jump out of the spinning trajectory of death the blade had created, giving him yet another precious instant to react.

Armless the wraith screeched, retreating. Trevor thrust the spear, catching it between the ribs. Its rib cage sprang open the swarm of insects coalescing into a black sphere of tar growing long tentacles that whipped out from its surface. In the center of this tar sphere a yellow eye sprang open as the sphere released itself from the rib cage, the bones of the wraith toppling backward lifeless, rattling as they piled on the damp earth.

The gorgon had moved to his left, the remaining two circling, in an ever-decreasing orbit toward him. He hurt, the adrenaline in his system was depleted, his wounds burned, there was a vacuous hunger in him as if his stomach was sucking him in, eating his bones and flesh as he collapsed in on himself, a dark star collapsing to black hole. His own energy was being used to create the explosive critical mass that would eventually swallow him.

He screamed as he twirled, dark blades flying outward, trying to push them back. He caught one black tendril from the cyclopean sphere, heard the clanging of a chain as he separated one talon from its link, and caught a few black snakes on the gorgon's head as he spun wildly out of control, using nothing but his fear and monstrous murderous instincts to drive him. The move caught them off guard, making them retreat just enough to create a gap between the white witch and gorgon which he sprinted through, running away from the temple and the circle of monsters toward the forest and Blood Mountain and Rakesh and the meadow, the saloon and its priest, his home. Running back in time before he knew what true darkness was, before he knew what real pain felt like, before he knew what it was like to have his humanity ripped from him.

The bell tolled, its waves ripping through and around him. Before him he observed the transformation as hell began to flux back to ghost village, the moss-covered cobblestones of the main street replaced those of the black earth, the old dilapidated buildings of the village replaced the obsidian black structures covered in darkta symbols, the gray hazy light of the moment before dawn replaced the blue-white lunar dark. As he looked down he saw his legs getting smaller, he felt closer to the ground, the strength going out of him, he looked up, his vision no longer as expansive or wide, he felt tired, cold, scared, scared to death. He needed to finish this. He had not come all this way to die. He stopped running; he had to or he would simply fall on his face. He did not want to turn; he was afraid of what he would see.

The gorgon and the white witch stood there facing him. Their transformations had begun, the temple behind them pulsed, vacillating from black demonic temple to dilapidated crumbling church that served as a house of worship to the ghosts inhabiting this long-dead town.

The gorgon's bow had transformed back to a stringed instrument that she plucked, her left hand running along the strings on the fret board. The crying whine of the tune pushed frigid needles into ears. The white witch was dancing and swinging her chains.

Gong … *How many was that?*

The curved blades of the pale witch's chains scooped up the black tar ball, becoming part of the swirling cyclone. She let the chains fly outward, screeching like an owl, a horrid sound. The black sphere sprang toward him, catapulting from the storm of the chains as they snapped straight, straining. The elliptical eye opened, staring at him. Fine lines of black flame radiated from the catlike iris, its tentacles pulsing black then white as it raced toward him.

Gong.

The sound waves rippled through space, the white witch was fingering herself seductively as the wave washed over her. The witch's form crumbled to ash as though a fire blast had reduced her instantaneously to dust. The gorgon's string popped, letting out an atonal squeak as her body disappeared in the ripple. The wave flowing over her body washed it into translucence.

The eye … closer … hypnotizing him. All he could do was watch. He knew it would obliterate him. Closer … Its pupil poised to engulf him. The ripple closed in, the tentacles turning to ash, the sphere smaller, smaller, tendrils of ash trailing its flight, a gossamer cloud of threads creating a vapor trail behind it. Trevor screamed. The eye engulfed him, the tentacles reached out toward him, they touched his face, one making its way into his open mouth. Blackness closed in around him, ash rained into his open mouth and he swallowed it, the world turned upside down as he stared up at the sky, pitched backward. He was falling … falling … falling …

Darkness.

Chapter 12

Trevor's eyes flutter. Sun rays caught in drops of dew crystallize surrounded by a golden halo sparkle in his vision. She is leaning over him, beautiful, radiant, covered in crystal orbs, her brown hair radiating gold in the sun that lights her from behind. She presses her lips to his right eye and whispers in his ear, lips brushing against his lobe, her breath warm, "Wake up."

He was on his back gazing up at the boughs and needles of the pine trees, the smell of smoke burning his nostrils as he heard the crackling of a fire to his right. He sat up. An old man with pale skin, deep lines and grooves covering his cheeks and forehead and piercing blue eyes smoldering from below the hoods of deep sockets sat in the dirt opposite Trevor, wearing dirty overalls over a flannel shirt. His white hair was flecked with dirt and looked greasy.

"Awake are ya. Don't be frightened I don't mean you any harm. I heard the bells and came to see what was happening and found you lying in the middle of the street. Brought you here. Dressed your wounds."

Trevor looked down at his bandaged torso and leg and felt the stitches along his jaw line to his ear where the gorgon's arrow had sliced. "Thank you."

The man nodded, his gaze unwavering.

"Who are you?"

"Just a guy with a sad story trying to make good. Revenge by substitution you might say, I guess," the old man said and shrugged. "Bell only tolls if the witch wills it. And then her minions are brought to bear. In some cases them ghost boxes in the tower vibrate too. Don't know what role they play in the whole transformation thing." He gazed into the distance looking over the town, seeming to picture the scene in his mind, biting his lower lip, hands shaking slightly. Trevor wondered what this man had seen. How many times had he witnessed what was unleashed by the tolling of the bell? He turned his gaze back to Trevor, his body seeming to ease as he did so. "You the first I seen to survive it."

Trevor shrugged. He had survived only by luck. He shivered as he remembered how the last ripple had transformed the deadly black sphere only a moment before it had unmade him, which made him question whether it had merely been good fortune or something the witch had a hand in. And what motivation would she have in rescuing him at a time when she could have ended him? Was she toying with him, saving him for something much more horrific?

"What is this village?" Trevor finally asked.

"Well for the likes of me and others like me it's where we gave up. We ceased our quest to chase the witch. She tortures us with her visions and her minions but we could no longer bear the cost of the chase."

"And what was the cost?"

"My soul. I found myself not caring what I had to do to get her and then found myself willing to do the very things that I'd refused to do for her which got me into the whole mess to begin with."

"Killing?"

"Yup. Killing, lying, cheating. I gave up at the killing point but just barely. Got so I couldn't remember what I'd lost or what I was chasing her for."

"Then why do you stay? Any of you?"

"I can only speak for me, but it was because I lost my way. I didn't belong nor deserve to return back to the world as though nothing happened. I felt like I deserved this." He paused and grinned crookedly. "And I secretly hoped another would come that would finish where I couldn't and maybe then I'd be released from that guilt."

Trevor grunted, not sure if he was that person. "And her minions stay here or are called here just to torture you?"

"Don't know for sure. They come with the bells so I 'spect that they are called by it from whatever dimension that bell opens. Hell, I guess. Truth is that the witch just likes to spread misery and if she can't spur us into chasing her she toys with us and when that stops being fun she'll kill us."

"And she prevents you from taking your own lives?"

"Ahh. Worse. She resurrects us. And her cruelty lies in us not knowing if she can continue to torture our loved ones from beyond the grave. That is what she tells us. It's how she gets us to go out looking for people like you."

"The man in the woods, who attacked me."

"Aye. Marvin was his name. You killed him I 'spect."

"I did."

"Don't think anything of it. 'Spect you'd kill me if I got in your way."

Trevor looked away and shifted uncomfortably, pain shooting up his side as he did so, grunting with a wince.

"I'm beyond judging, believe me. I've felt pain I didn't know was possible. So I ain't judging. But I 'spect you'll finish what I couldn't. And it needs finishing. That kinda evil must be killed."

"Regardless of the cost?"

He seemed to contemplate this, scratching his chin. "Cost of one man's soul for multiple ... Aye. Your soul for all those she's taken ... Aye. But I didn't say finishing means killing her necessarily. Is it fight fire with fire, one darkness erasing another, or can only light erase that darkness? That I don't know. But I guess for now I'd have to say no, not regardless of the cost. There is always a price to pay, it's the way of the universe, what provides balance, the dark equalizer. But there is also a price we shouldn't be willing to pay."

"Which is?"

"Only the individual being asked to pay up can decide that."

The man continued to stare at Trevor for a bit, seeming to measure him, coming to his own decision as to how he thought this would play out for Trevor. Having made up his mind, he shook his head slightly, "Anyway enough philosophizing. Get down to next steps. If you are going to go on then you need to go into the church during the transformation of the bell. So you need to kill her minions to get inside. Inside is a door which'll lead you to the land of the witch."

"And you know this how?"

"'Cuz she told me so."

"She told you?"

"Aye. You may be stronger than most, or darker—whatever—but as much as you believe you are chasing you are also being led."

Trevor put a hand to his right eye, the one bulging from his socket painfully.

"You may want to contemplate why that is." The old man said as though reading the question forming in Trevor's mind through his gesture. "So you got two and a half of those minions left to deal with, assuming you are going to continue your quest. Or else you stay, give up the chase, and go home. But of one thing I'm certain," he paused, staring into Trevor's eyes, placing emphasis on each word, speaking slowly, "You will never be free of her again. Even if you finish this, whatever that means I don't know, but even if you do, you may not be free. But if you don't finish it, I guarantee that you'll never be free."

With that they sat in silence, Trevor turning the conversation over in his head while replaying the battle of the previous night. There was no hope behind; he had already crossed that soul-crushing line when he had been willing to kill

Marvin in the swamp. And if the witch could really torture his family from beyond, then the only way they would be free was if he killed her. Was there a price he would not pay for that? She had taken everything from him. What more could she take? No! Certainly there was nothing left. Nothing to lose. The choice seemed obvious.

The moon was rising when Trevor finally made to leave. He had taken short naps during the rest of the day. During each Mary had visited him and he had wished he could have just stayed that way, in dream, enraptured by her face. In the last dream his son and daughter had joined her, each taking the time to kiss his cheek, and when he awoke he could feel the warm wetness of their phantom lips on his cheek.

The old man had fed the fire diligently, sitting quietly and watching over him. Trevor was sore but felt good in spite of his wounds. He took the blue crystals from his pack, stuffed them in the pipe, lit them with a branch and inhaled. He would need his mystical eye open for this battle. The drug also helped him forget the pain, diverting his attention with the hyperreality the world took on. Even now he could feel the dark force coalesce around him, fueling him. He then took the liquid poison that Rakesh had placed in a mason jar out of his pack. The by-product of the crystals was a powerful poison. He doubted it would kill the minions outright, but Rakesh had also told him it would change the characteristics of his weapons in the darkta and he needed every advantage he could get. Even in his transformed-by-the-bell darkta monster body he would not survive another beating like the one he had suffered. He poured the poison over the sharp edges and points of all his weapons and still had a small amount left in case he needed it in the future. He placed the sealed jar back in his sack, hefted his sword and spear, and took a deep breath. Already the fear of death was gone. There was the warmth of coming violence and the coldness of the darkta enveloping him.

"Goodbye and good luck."

Trevor shook the man's hand and nodded his thanks.

"I hope you find what you're looking for."

"I hope so too."

He checked his weapons one last time, lifted his rucksack, and walked away from the fire into the mist and the village beyond. The music began as soon as he entered the mist. That same depressing dirge in a minor key, worming painfully into his brain through his ears, in the same way the mist seemed to be rotting his innards through his pores. But now it was shy, the soft moan of an oboe and clarinet sounding all the more haunting for their absence.

Gong …

And so it began. But this time there was no surprise, he was ready for what was coming. He readied his spear, unsheathed his short curved sword as the doors of the black temple flew open, the black sphere emerging first, whining as it glided through the air. He ran toward the hill of corpses and ducked behind it; to his right was a black tree with talons covering its rough surface that shielded him in at least two directions. He did not want to meet his enemies in the open where the gorgon's arrows and the white witch's chains would make quick work of him. Narrowing their options would allow him to focus his defense and attack, something the previous encounter had taught him.

Gong …

The ripples hurtled through space, transforming the world. His vision morphed, his body expanded.

The gorgon emerged, slithering quickly across the front of the temple, her eyes searching out her prey.

Gong …

The white witch emerged, naked and dancing, her black flute spilling paranoia spores into the air, poisoning it.

Gong … Gong … Gong …

He waited, readying himself, breathing deeply of the darkta.

Gong… Gong… Gong…

The transforming ripples washed over him.

Gong … "Ten." Gong … "Eleven." Gong … "TWELVE!"

The world went silent for a moment as it completed its transformation into a dark hell. The white witch was fingering herself, the flute pushed between her breasts, the chains forming a coiling tempest around her body. The gorgon's bow flexed as she nocked an arrow, he could hear it creak in the dead air. The sphere had begun to circle scanning for prey. Trevor pushed himself against the heap of bodies, muscles coiling, waiting for the sphere to be close enough to attack. Its tentacles whipped around wildly, searching for purchase. It rounded the pile, hugging close to it, maybe believing he was hiding down one of the alleys, its eye scanning distantly.

Trevor uncoiled, leaping into the air, the eye never saw him, but the witch did and she let loose a horrific scream, too late to be a warning. Trevor thrust the black spear through the rear of the sphere the tip exiting its cyclopean yellow eye. It squirmed as it began to condense, being swallowed by the blade's dark gravity; the spear hummed, vibrating in and out of visibility, crossing dimensions unseen, and then appearing again in the darkta. The poison had birthed new powers in its metal, making it invisible as it phase shifted and fluxed from one reality to another. The spear would have the ability to pass through anything. For all he knew the sphere's shell might have been impenetrable had his weapon not been rendered more potent by the dark magic of the poison. The wound it inflicted caused the sphere to phase shift, unmaking it in the process. Each shift resulted in the sphere losing more of itself as it was sucked into multiple alternate dimensions, in effect tearing it apart and scattering the pieces throughout the multiverse until there was nothing left.

With the sphere gone he ran into the alley, hiding in the deeper shadows against the stone wall of one of the buildings. He wanted them to have to chase him. His mind was calm, focused; he saw the darkta with his mystic vision. He saw a space between the stones almost large enough to slip through and nudged it wider with his poisoned scimitar, which had also been transmuted to be a part of the darkta, operating within the realm of the mystic miraculous. He entered this dark space between worlds, allowing it to fold around him, cloaking him.

The blue moonlight cast the white witch's shadow upon the black earth, roots responded to her presence, becoming an extension of her will, seeking out her victim. But these extensions had no ability to peer through the cloak of the darkta. Her chains flew about, scraping roots, rock, the side of the buildings, the spiral fury forming a tempest whirling so quickly he could feel the pull of the vacuum it created.

She stepped into view. Her skin gleamed moonlight blue, paradoxically beautiful, shining like a star in the black landscape. Muscular legs flexed as she walked, hips twisting seductively as though this game of cat and mouse could be prelude to either love or violence. Her face turned in his direction, her eyes flashing more gold than yellow. She was staring right at him; the distance between them seemed to condense in the intensity of their stare. There was something so beautifully terrifying in her face, long silky black hair cascaded over her shoulders, a dark crown to the alabaster perfection of her skin. Her dark sensuality pulled at him. He knew her allure to be part of her trap. He felt himself stiffen and knew that the darkta would not protect or hide him soon. She was now only inches from him he could smell the sweetness of her skin. Her ecstatic beauty was disintegrating the layers of the spell he had cast about him, pulling apart the symbols into their base layers, revealing all that it hid.

He brought the scimitar up and brought his arm through the doorway. It appeared to her out of nowhere, the scimitar slicing across her throat, decapitating her, just as surprise registered in her eyes and the twitch of a sinister grin pulled at the corner of her lips. That odd expression froze on her face as though she had been turned to marble as her head rolled down the alley, her chains continuing to twitch against the alley walls like a fish pulled from a lake flapping in the dirt, dying as it tried to breath air. But the pale witch was not dead, at least not yet. She pulled on the chains flicking them with her wrist hoping that in her last moments she could inflict some violence and maybe even take him with her into whatever dark hell awaited them. Then at least they would have each other, lovers in darkness and death. Trevor brought his spear down through the hole in her neck, thrusting downward with all his might, the tip exiting her vagina and embedding into the stone of the alley trapping her. Her torso spun on the spear handle, continuing to search him out with her arms and her chains. Gore dripped down the spear, and as it pooled, the spear began to hum, the ground disappearing below her, a vacuous darkness forming. He held the top of the spear firmly, as the white witch was pulled into the black hole formed by the combination of the spear's magic and her own blood.

He was watching her fall into the pit when the gorgon's arrow hit his shoulder blade. It almost knocked him over with its force, and the thick muscles of his darkta body were the only thing that prevented it from going all the way through him. It stuck there painfully until he reached back with his opposite arm and pulled it free.

Trevor knew more arrows were coming for him, he could hear the creak of the bow and the sonic boom created by the shaft as it rocketed through the air. He lunged for the side alley as more arrows hit the stone of the building where he had stood just moments before. They exploded on impact, rock chips flying through the air, arrow shafts constructed from the bones of demons splintered, creating deadly projectiles that rained upon him. More than a few pierced the flesh of his arms, leg, and torso but none were long enough to go deep into the muscle. He grunted but kept moving putting one arm up to cover his eyes. He had no doubt that even a glancing blow from one of these pincers would blind him.

He had lost the spear, his hands slipping free of its handle as the first arrow hit his shoulder, but he still had the scimitar and his dagger. He gazed around the corner and he almost lost an eye as an arrow screamed within inches of his right eye, as though the archer had anticipated where her target would be in the next instant. The barbed blades at the tip of the arrow cut across his cheek and he pulled back, protecting himself behind the building. An instant later he ducked and ran across the alley, hoping the gorgon would not have the time to nock another arrow and aim before he made the far alleyway. Once in the alley he ran at full speed, coming to a stop at the first door. He had seen the swift slithering movement of the gorgon on the previous night and he knew he would not be able to outrun her or the arrows she was likely to launch blindly down the alley in a scatter pattern he would be unable to avoid.

Through the door was a small shop. Small glass bottles with cork stoppers and mason jars filled with ochre liquid filled the shelves. The air was damp and smelled of formaldehyde. As he stepped deeper into the shop and turned down one of the aisles, he saw shelves holding larger jars filled with eyeballs, snakes, human fetuses, and other small creatures or parts of creatures he had never seen before. Beyond that were some dried herbs, roots, and powders lying in the open, the fine powders and dust swirling about as the air was disturbed by his presence. At the back of the shop was a workbench with a pestle, bowl, scale, and some knives. As he came to the end of the aisle he saw the proprietor. He stood there shaking, holding a long butcher knife, the blade edge, recently sharpened, gleamed, smiling at him through the rust.

"Please make it stop," The man pleaded, his voice a whisper run over the sandpaper of his throat.

He was wearing a white smock covered in filth. It was yellow in most places, most likely from the formaldehyde, this the epicenter of the noxious aroma.

"Everything I did she made me do."

Trevor did not speak and he knew what must come next and dreaded it.

"I'm sorry." The man leapt at Trevor the blade raised over his head. His attempt was half-hearted at best. Trevor brought the blade of the scimitar down on his skull. On this nondeity it behaved as a conventional weapon. It did not separate the dimensions or form a gravitational anomaly, it simply cut through his skull from his crown to the bridge of his nose. The sound was sickening, as bone cracked and splintered, the wet coiled gray snake of his brain matter was bisected with a wet sucking sound as it swelled and pushed up out of the crack in his head and ran down his forehead. His eyelids blinked over cataract-clouded beige irises, his eyes crossed to stare at the blade and then closed as he fell backward. Trevor held onto the blade, yanking it from the man's head and taking skull and brain matter with it. The head smacked against the hard stone floor and exploded on impact. Thankfully the man was already dead, at long last, his wish fulfilled at least for the moment, provided that the witch did not see fit to resurrect him. Somehow he thought this unlikely, he could feel something in this death and could see the signs in the darkta as it moved over the body that this time death was final. In killing this man Trevor had done a good dead, at least that was what he told himself.

Trevor wiped the blade on his leg, giving the man and his death no further thought. He peered out the small circular window above the workbench. The gorgon was slithering past. He ducked silently to the left behind one of the aisle columns. She gave only a cursory glance through the window as she passed, moving swiftly, disappearing into the deeper darkness and mist at the far end of the alley. He opened the door at the back of the shop a crack and peered in the direction she had been traveling. She was gone and now he was behind her and could hunt her.

The mist was thick, the moon had made its appearance and reflected in the mist, funnels and rays of blue light twisted in the fog, disorienting him. He could only see a few feet in front of him at the best of times and the shifting light patterns dazzled his eyes, making it difficult to focus. His feet shuffled carefully across the ground, seeking solid purchase, the fog around his ankles hid the roots and rocks that threatened to trip him.

He could hear something slithering up ahead as he searched out her form in the mist. Closer. He raised his dagger, the moonlight swallowed by it caused the edge to burn electric blue, arcing and sparking, sizzling the air, the smell of ozone rising to his nose. He inched farther along the damp wall, listening to the sound of her slithering tail. She had stopped, waiting, unsure of which direction her target had gone. He approached the corner of the alley and stepped around cautiously. Before him lay a piece of flesh, probably pilfered from one of the corpses in the pile at front of the temple, pulled along the stone of the alley by a string that was attached to it creating the slithering sound he had been tracking. He followed the course of the string that was being pulled by ...

He put it all together too slowly, the arrow piercing through his trapezius muscle, just missing his neck. The impact was so forceful that it drove him into the wall; the arrow so sharp it actually pushed between the small fissures in the stone, trapping him there, his body convulsed against the smooth wet wall trying to pull free. The second arrow cut through his bicep right above the elbow and shattered his humerus on impact. He screamed out as he pushed against the wall with all his strength. He knew more arrows were coming. He fell as he released himself from the wall, the third arrow just missing his shoulder as he hit the ground, landing to the side of the slithering piece of decoy meat.

He could hear her sliding down the alley toward him, taking advantage of his fall to advance and finish him. He had dropped the dagger. He searched the ground for it and saw it lying five feet away on the stone. She was so close he could hear her breathing heavily, that wet slither more defined as he heard the coiling of the muscles in her tail, scales pushing through the sea of gore that covered the alley. He raised his head and searched the darkness and saw her jaundice eyes glowing in the dark, yellow areoles projected into the mist. The snakes upon her head were agitated and upright, hooked at the tip to search out prey, looking like rows of question marks. The question …

Fear gripped him, followed by confusion, and he intuitively knew he would be incapable of using the darkta in this state. He did not even have the time or strength to get up. Instead he barrel-rolled toward the knife. The first roll bent and then snapped the arrow shaft near his neck but not before pushing deeper through the muscle, the second had his arm screaming out for relief, but he pushed the pain aside, his eyes focusing on the dagger, his hands grasping for it, the awful sound of the gorgon's tail thundering and echoing in his ears.

The alley was narrow and her presence seemed to fill it from one wall to the other, her green skin gleaming beautifully, her features perfect, that same allure pulling him into its enchanting embrace. While his mind whirled, his body reacted without conscious direction, relying on the training Rakesh had embedded in his muscles; his hand grasped the handle of the knife as she raised her bow to deliver the killing shot, the arrow already nocked, the bowstring pulled taut, the bow creaking as it flexed. Time dilated and he could feel the neurochemicals drip into synapses, cascading electric impulses from one nerve to the next, pulsing, starting a neuronal fire in his brain. For one brief miraculous moment he could see the symbols of the darkta and formed the spell that caused his weapon to glow with black power. He threw the dagger at her, the blade expanded into a dimensional wormhole, her sulfur eyes widened in fear as she stared down the tunnel that ended in some dimension of horror and despair. He wondered if she could see the destination and if so how horrible that view must be if a creature that called this insane village home was in dread of such a place.

The gorgon opened her mouth to scream, sharp pointed teeth flashed from black gums, her forked tongue lolled from her mouth as it gaped, the tunnel of her throat formed a black pit. The transformed dagger buzzed, sparking in the air, flashing gray then jet-black. It struck her in the forehead, her mouth snapped shut, and she was pulled into the wormhole, the slime covering her skin sucked off as she was pulled through a hole too small for her large body, a tight birth into another dimension, the edges of the black ring dripped with her slime, falling in wet smacks and drips to the stones of the alley. She was gone. The black hole became a dagger again, hung suspended in the air for a moment, and then fell, clinking and clattering as it did so, the sound echoing on the walls. He had a moment to realize he had won before passing out, the cold stone covered in bile, mucus, and blood embracing him.

When he woke the moon was setting, and he knew he had to get to the black temple before the world returned to the daylight dimension in which the temple was a church. He pulled the arrow out of his neck. His dark body was quicker to heal. In his normal form he was sure that the wound would have taken weeks to heal but in his darkta body the process took only minutes, the blood flow slowing, the skin closing over the wound as the muscle repaired itself. He wanted to wait as long as possible before entering the temple, as he assumed that he would be returned to his normal body once he entered the dimensional portal and any unrepaired damage would take human time to heal, which could be weeks for some of the deeper wounds. He stood up.

Gong … "No!"

He began to run toward the temple, having no idea what would happen if he did not reach the portal before the final toll. Would the portal close forever? Would he have to wait until the next night? Would the whole sequence start all over again, an eternal return until he accomplished his goal in full? He did not want to find out.

Gong … Would it ring twelve times? Had it been twelve the night before?

Gong … Tolling faster now, just as it did on the outset.

He entered the temple as the fourth gong sounded.

Inside the black walls glowed with the sigils and spells he had seen the night before, etched with surgical precision into the onyx-colored stone. The soft glow lit an intricate mosaic floor made of fine tiles and glass—red, blue, black, white, opal, gold, colors he had no name for, as if created just to display the color palette of this world, the rainbow of the darkta. If there was some scene or pattern in the display he could not discern it, making its chaos all the more beautiful through its lack of purpose.

Gong …

The sound was amplified within the walls, echoing and rattling in his chest. At the rear of the temple were two pillars: one was alabaster white with intricately carved black symbols covering its surface; and to its right was its dark brother, a black column with white symbols. Between them flashed the portal. Inside this dark mass floated a galaxy of stars, a dazzling, swirling storm of white, red, yellow, and blue that flashed, exploded, and erupted with dust clouds and particles shooting off in all directions, white dwarfs collapsing, and supernovas exploding. Trevor's focus locked on a white star that exploded in a flash of blue, sending ripples that flew across the system, blowing stardust across the expanse. The dust settled, coalesced; the stars burned brighter for an instant, expanding outward, a spiral with a dark center. So dark. A void so black he had no words to describe it.

His right eye twitched. Pulled.

Gong …

He could not wait, the pull in his eye insisted that it would be ripped from his skull if he did not comply with the will of this dark universe and the black god at its center.

He jumped into the portal. He felt an icy cold hand embracing him, tendrils of ice worming its way into every neuron, every muscle, every chamber of his heart. Lights flickered as he entered the pattern and flow of the downward spiral toward the dark center. Dread flooded into him, fear of meeting the dark god of this universe pulsed through his veins. He picked up momentum, the ride became dizzying, his stomach lurched, but it was beautiful; even in that frigid cold he felt at peace, the eye guiding him down the spiral to the epicenter. The closer he got, the more squeezed he felt, as though he were being shoved into a small box that continued to get smaller.

When he reached the center it felt as though the box he had been squeezed into had been thrown off a cliff, dizzying weightlessness, then the box around him collapsed, crushing him, and in the next instant he was tumbling, expanding, stretching. The tumbling increased in speed and intensity as he was pulled apart, his limbs flying away, his torso, his legs, his arms spread out over an ocean of black.

Silence. Nothingness. He floated darkly, perfectly.

Suddenly he was spiraling again, his limbs smashing into each other, reconnecting. Then the centrifugal force of the spiral tore him apart into tiny fragments and he became one with the sea of darkta, lost in the ocean of space. Flushed down the toilet of the gods. Nothing. Everything.

Chapter 13

Trevor's eyes opened slowly, a face hung above him. Mary, he thought, but her face was no longer crystal clear. Her features were no longer etched in the stone of his memory; they floated listlessly, attempting to coalescence into a recognizable face. She leaned in, lashes trembling against his cheek, her silky, warm lips brushing against his ear as she whispered, "Wake up, Trevor."

His eyes fluttered, his lids felt like steel grates crashing together, heavy, difficult to lift, but he pushed them up. He was lying on his side on the rocky shore of a river, its surface an inky black. The small, smooth pebbles he was lying upon were dark gray and black. Across the black liquid expanse was a thick gray mist; forms that might have been dead trees with skeletal branches wavered in and out of existence. The mist thinned slightly and Trevor believed he saw the rectangular boxes of a ghost-talk tower. The mist thickened again, clouding his view. To his right and left was a river, its darkness disappearing into impenetrable walls of fog. His right eye spasmed letting him know that his destination lay across the expanse.

He closed his eyes, suddenly tired and cold. Tired of this battle. He tried to picture his wife's face, feel the silkiness of her hair, the taste of her lips, the smell of her skin, and he could not; in that instant he wanted to quit. To cry and admit he had lost.

There is nothing but deathly silence as he sits staring across the dark river, wondering how he should cross and whether the darkness will allow such a thing or will merely swallow him. He does not care. It needs to end one way or the other. He hears the distant slap of something hitting the water, slow, rhythmic, moving closer. The black bow pushes through the wall of mist, seeming to rise organically from the inky pitch of the surface of the river as if formed from the same substance. The boat's skin is the consistency of thick liquid, black tar sculpted into a hull, skimming across the deeper black of the water. The boat is long and narrow, its hull sweeping upward, curling at the end into the swirl of a question mark. The source of the rhythmic slapping is a single oar dipping into the ink, dragged backward, and then repeating. No ripples or wake accompany the displacement of water by either boat or oar, and he realizes it may not be water at all. His mind had conveniently chosen a word symbol for what he had seen, but there was nothing he now saw that told him he was standing on the banks of a body of water. The only evidence was the sound of the oar. But it could be a moat of emptiness, the sound he heard nothing more than the oar slapping against the hand of nothing.

Then he looked from the oar to the creature manipulating it. It had a large human shape, not as tall as the colossus but taller than an average human, but it was not constructed of flesh and bone and had only cursory facial features. It was cobbled together from mud, stone, sticks, leaves, and moss. His grandfather would have called it a golem, a creature composed of earth but created and held together by sorcery. As it approached he saw that a black river stone formed one eye, a mushroom cap, the other. Roots served for its spidery veins and neurons, pulsing darkta energy through its torso, which was held together by thicker sticks and vines that acted as a skeleton, holding the mud together. Other sections were patched with wet green moss or grass that knitted other sections of its flesh together. The mud that acted as its skin was not brown but black and gray, rich topsoil and compost mixed with ash. The form had been knit using material from across the river, the land of the dead, the land of the witch.

There was no sound to its movements. The whole scene took place in utter silence, save the rhythmic rowing. Trevor knew instinctively that it was here to carry him to the far shore, where he knew the witch was waiting. He leaned over the edge, peering into the black, and saw that he cast no reflection; the substance, whatever it was, swallowed his image. There was nothing but abyss. He seemed drawn into it, enveloped by it, his consciousness slipping into the darkness. Whatever it was, it was not water. He stood on a precipice staring into the void, its black fingers reaching out for him to pull him into its insane embrace.

He was leaning farther and farther over the abyss, unable to stop himself. Then there was a hand on his shoulder, gently but insistently pulling him back. He glanced at his shoulder to see his wife's thin smooth fingers pulling at his shoulder. "Not yet," she whispered into his ear. He could sense that Jake and Lydia were there as well, but he did not want to turn, there were tears in his eyes and he knew that if he turned to look at them it would all be over, that he would give up, that he would let the darkness claim him or would turn back, go back over Blood Mountain and join Rakesh, maybe go all the way home, lost, afraid, broken.

He shook his head. No. He had to go on.

The boat pulled up next to him. The face of the golem turned to stare at Trevor with its black eye of stone. His right eye spasmed again, letting him know that he needed to cross; its pull was slightly more insistent this time. He moved to get in the boat and the golem put his hand out to stop him.

Trevor studied it, leaves and moss embedded in the dark muck of its skin, branch tips poked through its fingertips, wood knots exposed as it flexed its fingers, palm up waiting. Trevor prayed it did not want to shake his hand or help him aboard. He dreaded the thought of touching it. The image of Cyrus, the sniveling store owner in Krull who had tried to extort him for information, rose in his mind. He had made the same open-palmed expectant gesture and Trevor knew that the golem was waiting to be paid for taking him across. He put his rucksack down and opened it, searching from something to give that he felt he no longer needed. He handed over his flint and steel dropping them in its palm. As he did so his right eye twitched, and he knew the moment before the golem turned his open palm upside down, letting the objects drop into the abyss, that it was the wrong thing. He needed to part with something dear to him. There was only one thing he could think of. He reached into the bottom of the sack and pulled out the tin containing the ashes of his home. It was the last thing he had that tied him to the shore of this existence, to his old life, to the old Trevor. He did not want to give it up, somehow he knew it was the anchor preserving what was left of his humanity. His eye twitched again, this time letting him know this was the correct payment. Trevor swallowed hard and placed the tin in the golem's outstretched hand. It opened the tin and then shook the ash onto its palm and pushed its palm to its breast, the ash absorbed into its muddy flesh. The golem gestured for him to board the boat. The boat did not tilt or creek as Trevor stepped in. The golem began paddling again, directing the boat toward the opposite shore.

As they approached the far shore, Trevor turned one final time now that he knew there was no way for him to get back, no way for him to change his mind. They stood there on the opposite bank of the river, the mist beginning to thicken around them. They were waving, Jake smiling as he always did, Lydia sitting on the shore curling and uncurling her fingers in a goodbye gesture, and Mary, radiant in the gray, that halo surrounding her, lighting her from behind and within, was smiling. And he knew this was the last he would ever see of them. Beyond this was hell, it was an evil place where no light or beings of light could enter.

He waved and turned toward the approaching shore and as he stepped from the boat to touch the hard beige stone he felt his heart break, felt his soul slipping into darkness, hiding somewhere deep within so that it could not be discovered, so that the Coma Witch could not kill it. More than one line had been crossed on this journey.

The boat and the golem continued on, eternally traversing the abysmal river, and when he looked back he saw nothing but mist. He was alone, alone in a way he had never experienced before.

The tug on his eye was stronger here. It would lead him through this wasteland to her.

He headed into the fog, going in the direction his eye led him. The ground beneath his feet was crystallized, with various hues of brown and beige, shot through with stripes of rust, orange, amber, and red. The air was thick with the rotten egg smell of sulfur. There were holes in the ground where thick hot steam gushed into the air, even feet away he could feel its heat, smell the poison it spilled into the air. It was a toxic environment, a fitting setting for the witch.

And then he saw the towers. Not just ghost-talk towers but others that were even larger and taller, forming large crosses that held thick rusty cables that ran through the air from one to another. The rusted surfaces had also been crusted over with dripping crystals. Steam vents near them had covered them with minerals and toxin-rich steam that over the years had hardened, creating a patchwork of rust and crystal that looked very similar to tree bark, giving them the appearance of enormous trees. Large mesh bowls with concave surfaces pointed at the sky. Each had a long spear pointing upward toward the heavens. Everywhere he looked there were wires, crosses, bowls, tubes, and ghost-talk towers forming objects and patterns he had never seen anywhere else in his travels.

As he slowly made his way through the petrified forest he remembered a legend he had heard growing up of an island the ancients had created to harness all the power of their techknowledgies. The sun fields, the huge windmills, and power stations had all of their sorcerous energy directed to the island. They had built it far from the rest of the world to test out new and powerful magic. This island was where they had created the giants and other beings, performed genetic experiments, and manipulated matter. Here they had developed the ability to mold creatures from the earth like the golem and created the muties and colossi. He wondered whether maybe this was where the witch had been made or born, if that was why she had chosen this as her home.

There was a vibration that could be felt in the ground, heard in the air, felt in his bones, galvanizing the surface of his skin, making the hairs on his arms stand up. The techknowlegies here still had power and had not completely run down. He then came to a large tube buried in the earth. He estimated that it had to be at least twenty feet across. A channel had been cut into the earth, the large tube laid within it. There were knobs and wheels and vents across its surface at regular intervals. There was a curve to its path and he imagined that it formed a large circle.

An image of his grandfather rose before him, his face hovering before him in the mist, his deep blue eyes staring at him intently. That deep sonorous voice that he had always loved to listen to spoke from the disembodied floating head. "The ancients created large wheels made of huge steel pipes. They were many, many miles in circumference. The ancients would accelerate matter through these pipes in opposite directions and then smash them together to form the dark matter that they used to power their sorcery and magic machines. The ghost-talk towers and their other techknowlegies use this power to operate. And the ancients became obsessed with having more and more of it." He paused and took a toke from his pipe, breathing out the thick tobacco smoke slowly. "But they did something else even more sinister with these wheels. The most gifted and arrogant of the ancients would smash matter together in an attempt to uncover Mother Nature's secrets, stripping off her robes to reveal the very mysteries that made her beautiful. They left her naked and raw reducing her to a dark hag forced to fight for her life. And she did fight back, she fought back with terror and fear and darkness, and that darkness spread over the world.

"They had wanted to control something that was out of control and in the process created the poison that killed them."

Trevor had been enthralled as a young boy by the stories of the ancients but he had never thought of them as more than clever fictions passed on from generation to generation, embellished and expanded upon by each new generation of storytellers. The ancients had existed; that was obvious. The refuse of their broken techknowledgies littered the world. Those that still worked were useful but not enough that anyone would try to fix them or fuel them when they ran down. Techknowledgy, he had been taught, was an evil that once dead should be allowed to stay dead. Being here on the legendary island showed him that these stories had been true. Grandfather had said that the island was a circle of hell that had been devoted to the sorcery of making gods of men. But they only succeeded in revealing and angering the more ancient gods that had lain hidden within the mysteries of darkta and illukta. The ancients had unleashed the very monsters that would end their reign. Was the witch a god? Was she the mother stripped of her clothes, raped by the ancients, and reduced to a dark hag? Or was she a creation of the darkta experiments?

Trevor scanned in all directions and was sure that if the fog cleared he would see the ancients' towers, structures, and cables stretching out to the horizon. As he turned back around, his eye tugged insistently, telling him that his destination was at the hub of the gigantic wheel used to smash matter and reveal its secrets.

Trevor took a running leap from the edge of the channel, landing on the slippery curved surface of the huge tube. He had to steady himself with his hands before standing upright. He looked across the patchwork of steel and crystallized minerals. In some places arcane symbols he did not recognize were etched or painted on the steel surface. They meant nothing to him. With nothing else to see he jumped to the other side of the ditch and continued to walk in the direction of the hub, his eye leading him.

As he walked he would occasionally detect motion out of the corner of his eyes, but when he turned in that direction there would be nothing. In the mist he only saw vague shapes. He was hungry and tired and his throat burned with the effort of breathing the noxious air. His head swam, his vision wavered, and he felt faint. Every time he was tempted to rest he pictured his family's heads on the table, the witch's evil laughter, the people he had met who had begged him to finish this, and he pressed on. He knew if he stopped to rest he would never get up again, so he shuffled his feet relentlessly. One foot in front of the other, a mantra and routine that became his whole focus.

The moon was rising when his legs began to cramp. The technoscape was rendered even more haunting in the light of a moon that glowed rusty red, the steam and mist seemed on fire in its glow. Shadows lengthened and the petrified iron and steel trees became giant skeletons with claws that sought him out, that hungered to pull the flesh from his bones. Finally, his legs would move no more. He fell to his knees on the hard, smooth, damp ground. It was like smooth marble with ripples—a waterfall frozen in midstream.

He glanced in the shallow pool, the still water offering a mirrored surface. His hair was long, hanging in greasy unkempt strands, shrouding a much thinner face covered in a thick beard. His face had once been round but now it had hard lines around his eyes and nose, his cheekbones jutted out. He felt his face, exploring the deeper pockets that once had been full rosy cheeks. His reflection was that of a woodland ascetic who had deprived himself of all comforts to find spiritual bliss. He barely recognized the face in the water. Was he a mystic in search of a dark revelation or was he the questing knight in search of justice?

"Why am I here?" he whispered.

"It was your choice, dearie."

Her voice rose from the watery pool, ripples forming on its surface, sending the shrill vibrations through the air, interfering and combining with the tremors that resulted from the hum of the towers, their cables, and the large matter-smashing wheel.

"Did I choose?" His voice sounded so loud. His throat ached as he spoke.

"Aye. You did. Your hate has blinded you, but mayhaps you have found epiphany after all. The darkta is part of that."

"Part of what?"

"ALL. EVERYTHING. You've felt it I know you have ..."

"Felt what ...?"

"The truth, cully. The truth of what we are, why we are."

The pool went silent, returning to glass. He could not move. He was exhausted. He let his eyes close for a moment ...

His eyes opened, his body wracked with pain. It seemed impossible to move. He had not seen the darkta since coming to the island. He tried to open his mystic eye but could not, the effort sent stabs of pain into the center of his head. Keeping his natural eyes open seemed painful and the black eye was pulsing. Try as he might he could not see the darkta. He lay back for a moment. He could not tell whether his muscles were twitching or the ground was moving below him. There was a deep vibration that made the ground feel like a dull moving ocean, the waves rippling beneath him, carrying him as he floated upon its sluggish waves. The red moon at its zenith, the mist coalescing around his vision, forming a series of concentric red rings. For a moment there was peace, there was beauty. He closed his eyes briefly and when he did the sea became turbulent, the shaking intensifying, making him feel sick.

He sat up. He could think of only one thing to do. He took the last of the blue crystals from the box in his rucksack and pushed them into his pipe. He took the gas lighter Rakesh had gifted him and pulled the trigger. A small flame appeared at the end and he carefully brought the wavering tongue of fire to the crystals as he breathed in slowly and deeply. The smoke burned his throat and lungs but he held onto it before breathing out. He put the pipe and lighter back in his rucksack and then took out the dark liquid poison that swirled at the bottom of the Mason jar.

The drug was working already he could feel the cold dagger poking dully at the bridge of his nose, coaxing his dark eye open. He took out his weapons: two curved scimitars and the dagger with the serrated blade. He smeared the gray poison over the surface of the weapons and they began to pulse with darkta energy. At the center the blades were pitch black, the vacuum of deep space. As energy was pulled into this gravitational anomaly, the orbiting matter flashed, making the edges of the blade gleam from red to pink to white; sparking and crackling with darkta, humming as he slashed at the air, swallowing more energy.

At that moment a screech owl let out a high-pitched scream, harbinger to the end, scarring the air. Pools bubbled and the crystal flows, stalagmites, and stalactites began to vibrate at a higher frequency, creating a sound like that of an organ that had all its keys pressed simultaneously; a cacophony that was disorienting and made his ears ring. The combination of drug, noxious fumes, ringing ears, and hazy red light made him dizzy.

The owl screeched again and as it did the witch rose from the shallow pool in front of him, dressed in a dark silk robe that shimmered in the red light of the moon. Her skin was a smooth radiant milky white. Long jet-black hair hung down, covering her face. The owl screeched and she flung her head up, hair tossed backward to reveal a face that was unfamiliar. It was not the face of evil that had tortured him these many months. This face was beautiful, sublime. The face enraptured him. As he gazed deeper he could still see the shadow of the features that identified her as his enemy, the Coma Witch. This quest had transformed him into a despairing, violent, hateful ascetic, while she had been transmuted into a beautiful dark goddess. There was still the bulging left eye, black globe turning within the alabaster perfection of her face. Darkta spells were etched on its surface, glimmering like coals in the reflected moonlight. She sprung at him, arms outstretched, grabbing for his throat.

He slashed upward with his dagger, the hissing red blade screaming as he sliced across her wrist. She immediately pulled back placing her hand over the wound and staring up at him, that sinister smile broadening. "Aye, you've done it now apprentice. I can feel the dark poison entering my blood. Now there is no turning back for you." Her voice was velvety smooth, seductive. Gone was the crackling cackle that had rattled his teeth. She was slithering backward and he moved toward her trying to capitalize on his advantage. He raised the humming blade again, white-red arcs flashing across its surface. She raised the edges of her robe covering half her face and vanished, pulling a darkta spell and slipping between the empty spaces. He tried to manipulate the fabric of the darkta to follow her trail and slip through the same holes, but she had sealed the passage behind her. It made no difference. The eye was pulling him and he let it lead. It would not be far, he intuitively knew this from the subtle vibrations that quaked across the surface of his black, engorged eye. He ran across the slippery crystal flows with ease, his dark body more powerful and sure-footed, finding safe passage over the hazardous terrain.

In the darkta the technoforest was transformed into a large musical instrument. Insect-like creatures with sharp claws or rows of pincer-like teeth crawled across the crystal branches and trunks, their metallic limbs and teeth clicking on the surfaces, echoing, striking notes and chords. A symphonic cacophony rose around him. The monks of the dark isle had come to chant. Their haunting melody enveloped him as he ran. The screech owl beckoned, its high-pitched scream echoing and intensifying within the bowels of the large instrument. Every structure tied to every other one, each note added to that before it, the structure intensifying the symphony, pushing him forward.

He ran, for how long he could not discern. A group of small, black, red, and silver creatures that reminded him of salamanders, snakes, fish, crabs, and lobsters followed him, they were the muties, failed experiments and discarded monsters of the ancients. Their claws, teeth, feet, and tails formed the notes of the dirge that led him forward. As the creatures scrambled over stalactites, crystallized branches, and earth, their appendages made the crystals vibrate, forming notes that were then amplified by the larger instrument of the environment.

The center of the circle formed by the matter-smashing tube was his destination. Everything was confirming it—his eye, the music, the creatures, all leading him there. It was the hub of this wheel, the hub of this world, the place where all journeys ended.

He slowed his pace as he approached the center. There was a large hole with rust-colored stone steps leading below the surface, beyond that was darkness. When he stopped walking the world went quiet, the creatures stopped their chant. He stood looking down, knowing he had to descend. There was no going back now and if he did not move soon the eye would pull itself from its socket. There was fear at the pit of him. Some unknown intuition was telling him this would not end the way he thought. This had started as simple revenge, or he had thought it was simple. But it had become more complex than he could ever have imagined. And if he could not imagine the path that had brought him to this spot, how much less equipped was he to determine or see or even theorize its outcome.

He glanced around at the sea of creatures surrounding him, waiting like supplicants for their prophet to speak or act. There was nothing for him to say, so he took the first step and began his descent below the surface. By the sixth step he had disappeared from view but the creatures did not move. They sat and waited, not knowing why but knowing they must.

Once the darkness settled in and the realm above disappeared, a deeper darkness enveloped him before giving way to surrealist visions. He stood near the top of a long flight of steps that ended far below him. From here it did not seem as though they had a destination, they just ended in empty space. In the darkness surrounding him floated islands of place and time, snow globes depicting other worlds locked in a perpetual cycle. There he beheld pieces of heaven and hell, alternate dimensions and alien landscapes.

In one globe there stood a huge dark tower with millions of rainbow-colored strands entering its base. A dark figure stood upon a high balcony and turned to stare at him coldly. In another there were tall buildings reaching toward the sky. Two pillars that rose above the rest were burning, black smoke rising into the air. In a third a mushroom cloud was rising behind a flash of white-hot light that turned to red and orange flame, the black cap of the cloud looming over a dead world.

Everywhere he looked he saw something new. Something unknown, disturbing. Each scene was one of pain, desolation. They depicted various explorations of the agony caused by a system bent upon its own destruction. What dark demonic deity had created such a menagerie of worlds? He saw a man hanging from a cross, men burned alive in chambers while others in black uniforms stood and watched, weapons spit deadly projectiles at innocent women and children, their blood staining the earth red. His heart ached and he closed his eyes, not wanting to see anymore. When he opened them again he focused only on the steps, not wanting to look up and gaze into some new horror. He continued his descent slowly, one step at a time, for what seemed like miles.

When he reached the last step he raised his eyes to see what he knew in his heart he must see, the witch's hut. He grinned. Dark trees loomed above the stone hut and thatched roof with thick gray smoke rising from the chimney, smelling of rot and sulfur. He knew now that the witch's hut existed in all worlds. It was the entrance to the tunnel of doors; it was the empty space behind all things. It was dark, shimmering, as if seen through a haze, fluxing. Fear welled up in him, he was shaking, sweat dampened his forehead, even his darkta body felt weak in the presence of this odd monument marking the entrance into misunderstanding, paradox, fear, disdain, and pain. He opened the door slowly. It was almost exactly as he had remembered it from his last visit here but his view was different. What had been on the right-hand side before what now on the left. The shift did not make sense to him. There was a rocking chair creaking slowly, some ghostly visitor causing it to sway back and forth. The room smelled of must and smoke, reminding him of arcane knowledge, old books. He scanned the shelves of leather-bound books with thick cracked covers, the letters worn from their spines. There were parchment scrolls the color of bone tied in cylinders with leather thongs. On other shelves were mason jars filled with liquids of various hues, gold, silver, black, purple, orange, yellow; eyes or other alien things he had no name for floated in ocher liquid. Powders and small vials littered the lower shelves. It was exactly as he had seen it the previous time but seen at a different angle, his perspective revealing things he had not noticed previously. There was something quaint in the surroundings, as if he had entered the home of an old scientist. It was how he had pictured the dwelling of religious hermits or great inventors or alchemists. It felt strangely like … home. It felt right in his mind, his body reacting to it, the terror suddenly gone. At the opposite end of the room was a door. And suddenly he remembered, when he had looked through the darkta the last time he had encountered her house. He understood now why his perspective was different. He was entering through the hearth.

"Oh my God," he whispered. He had entered from the opposite side when he had been brought to the hut from the woods; the creature he had seen emerging from the hearth had been him, the darkta him, the now him. But how was that possible? Had he gazed into the future to see his future dark self emerge through the hearth? He remembered how that image had terrified him, how it had made his blood curdle. A form appeared in the rocking chair. It was her, naked, gleaming, beautiful. Her left eye was a normal size now and he realized suddenly that his had grown. It hurt, twitching spasmodically, shooting pain through his skull.

She studied him with eyes of clear blue. The only blemish on her was the cut on her wrist, which stood out, an angry red at the edges but black in the center where the poisoned blade had broken the skin. She grinned sensually at the sight of him, spreading her legs slightly, that mysterious cavern between her legs opening for him, pink warmth surrounding the dark enigma. He damned himself as he became aroused. He tried to conjure the image of his wife and to his horror found her features superimposed over that of the witch, a phantom whose features swam around her, not quite coalescing, like a reflection in shifting water, but then it fixed itself and he could no longer remember any face beyond that which held his attention now.

She flashed a seductive, knowing smile as a convulsion rippled through her body, starting at her head as she shook it from side to side and then the rest of her body followed until the quiver ran out the bottom of her feet, the poison beginning to take its effect.

"So ya killed me. How does it feel?"

It was only now that he fully realized he had completed his vengeance and he was horrified again when he felt nothing for it. His mystic eye opened. The darkta was shifting, he could feel its weight, its gravity. It had been pulling at him across the miles, the headaches, the pain, but now it was surrounding him, opening him up, he felt its power, it was a force of nature, not judgment, not evil, it was just—the dark. It delivered its revelation through loss, sorrow, pain, and anger, and it was powerful. But it could also act as a healer, removing that which could not be transformed, that which needed to be destroyed and leveled in order to be reborn. It was a blind beast, a force of nature. It was apocalypse. It was blessed extinction for that which had run its course and would now be reduced to food for the next iteration, the next form to attempt to reach the next rung on the ladder toward the enlightenment of illumika.

"You see it now, don't you?"

"See what?" He had seen so much.

"The truth, apprentice."

His mind screamed at her second use of the word "apprentice" but it was not his first concern. "What truth?"

"The truth and power of the darkta? There is nothing to fear in it. Its chaos is that which allows light to shine and it is powerful at stripping away facades and illusions." She shuddered again, "Now finish me off. I've completed my turn on the wheel."

Through clenched teeth Trevor spit, "For what you've done I'd prefer to let the poison kill you slowly." As if in response to his words, her body twitched and convulsed violently. This time a cry escaped her throat and Trevor allowed himself a sadistic smile.

"Then you don't see the truth of the darkta. You've allowed your pain and fear to hide it."

"One more lesson then?"

Somehow she conjured enough energy to open a door in the darkta and pull him through it into a dark tunnel that he flew through at great speed. Thousands of doors flashed by before he came to an abrupt stop and was forced through one of the doors.

Beyond the door the sun is bright. Dandelion seeds fly and circle in a gentle breeze. The sun has begun to set. He knows immediately where and when he is. The witch is trying to anger him, make him relive his mistake so that he will oblige her last wish and kill her. He steadies himself. There is a paradox to the experience. The memory seems so distant, as though it had occurred to someone else, yet at the same time feels like yesterday, raw and visceral. His conversation with Kyle must have just ended because the boy is walking off into the woods, away from home. He remembers how peculiar that had seemed to him at the time. How it had made him feel uneasy.

He expected that now he would be forced to follow his previous path back to the scene of horror waiting for him at home but instead he is led by his awful eye to follow Kyle.

The day is turning gray. Kyle is walking quickly, with purpose and direction. Trevor feels more ill at ease. First there had been the boy's surprise when Trevor had called out to him, as though he had been caught doing something he was not supposed to be doing. Then there was the fact that after Trevor said goodbye Kyle had walked farther into the woods. This had all bothered him at the time, but in the wake of the scene he had uncovered at home, he had forgotten it and it had been buried in his memory until now. But now he knows something is definitely wrong and that something bad is about to happen. Something that would not have happened had he killed the boy right then and there as he was supposed to.

Over Kyle's shoulder he sees a girl wading in the stream, the babbling sound of the water over rocks making her deaf to Kyle's quick approach. He has pictured this very thing, his step does not falter, he has planned this and Trevor suddenly realizes Kyle has done this before. His actions are too sure. Too precise. Rarely can one dream or think of something and then just do it without hesitation. Trevor knows this all too well. How many times had he dreamed of slitting the boy's throat only to hesitate and give up when the time arrived? Trevor can tell that this has not only been practiced in Kyle's mind, he has committed a similar act before, adding confidence to every step.

Kyle pulls a hunting knife from the sheath that had been tucked in the back of his pants, running up his spine. He hits her in the back of the head with the metal handle and she topples over. She is young, so young, Jake and Kyle's age, twelve, no more than fourteen. Curly red hair, freckles, pail complexion, pretty. She struggles as Kyle straddles her and mounts her. His knees pin her flailing arms, his ass sitting on her chest making it difficult for her to breath. Her sundress tears as she struggles but she is unable to unseat him or roll him off her. Her eyes blaze as Kyle's darken, he places the blade against her throat. She stops moving, tears well up in her eyes, replacing the rage. They look into each other's eyes. She knows she is going to die. She does not beg to be spared. The scene is eerily quiet, as if the brook, birds, and forest have all stopped to watch this momentous scene. He slices her throat, blood jutting from her neck. She does not make a sound as her blood sprays all over Kyle, the light dying in her eyes. Kyle lifts his head to the sky, a look of ecstasy on his face.

Trevor is crying, shaking. This is what he had sacrificed his family for?

He is being pulled backward through the tunnel of doors.

He shuts his eyes and when he opens them again he is staring at the witch.

"Not what you expected now was it?" There is no smile, no hint of sardonic humor in her voice. "Wasn't what I expected when I was taught a similar lesson so long ago. But I still remember."

Trevor pulled the dagger from its scabbard; it glowed blackly. Now she smiled. He sank the blade into her forehead. She seemed to shrink. There was no noise; silently she was unmade, curling up into an origami ball and then gone. The blade then pulls him into its swirling center.

He is infused by the darkta. It whispers to him softly like a lover, and suddenly he knows all, the answers to his questions are revealed. Total darkness. It lasts for a moment or an eon, he cannot tell. Time is irrelevant. The globes of frozen moments fall about him like raindrops, hundreds of thousands of dark moments falling through the abyss. He, the black necromancer, sits upon a black throne woven from the strands of the darkta, hovering in the void, beholding the myriad islands of time as he waits for the darkta to command him. What was Trevor is gone. Now there is only the darkta sorcerer. Now there is only the shadow waiting for light to reveal it.

The End

About The Author

Brian White, author of *The Strands* and *In the Shadow of the Witch*, lives in New Jersey with his wife and two daughters. His writing is inspired by progressive heavy metal music, philosophy and mysticism.

Learn more about the author at:
www.darkrevmedia.com

Or contact him directly at:
brianwhite@darkrevmedia.com